RETURN TO INIS MÓR

Brian O'Raleigh

Copyright

Copyright Brian O'Raleigh – 2023
Print Edition

All rights reserved. No part of this publication can be reproduced, stored in retrieval systems, or transmitted, in any form or by any means, (electronic, mechanical, photocopying, recording, or otherwise), without the prior written permission of both the copyright owner and the publisher of this book.

The characters in this book are fictitious. Any resemblance to real people, living or dead, is purely coincidental.

Return Inis Mór

O'Raleigh – Brian
November 2023

Dedication

I dedicate this book to my wife, Kadek.
Without her love and encouragement,
It would not have been possible.

There are four harbors between Heaven and Earth
Where souls are cleansed
The Paradise of Adam, Rome, Aran, and Jerusalem
No Angel who ever came to Ireland to help Gael or Gaul
Returned to Heaven without first visiting Aran.

Cormac mac Cuilennáin
King of Munster – Bishop of Cashel
Died 13th September 908 AD

PROLOGUE

Saint-Goustan – Brittany

"For he was the cook and captain bold,
And mate of the Nancy brig."

William Gilbert

LEAVING SAINT-GOUSTAN TORE my heart out. Giselle standing on the wharf, still and straight. The words between us hollowed out by sorrow. I'd tried to talk to her about getting back together, but she'd avoided any commitment.

"This is not the time, Conor," she said, "My mother is dying."

I bent to kiss her, but she moved her head slightly, and our lips barely touched.

"Safe home," she turned. "Call me when you arrive, Tristan will be worried."

I went aboard and slipped the for'ard lines. And as I raised the foresail, a breeze caught *Erin*, and she turned her bow towards the open sea. I glanced back, Giselle was standing at the top of the stairs, staring down. Her long, dark hair pulled back into twin curling braids: her stance proud, almost arrogant. I went to turn back, but there was no point, we'd talked it over a dozen times.

"You can't stay, Conor, there's no work for you here; you

have no French. The only way you could help is to go back to Inis Mór and take that boatbuilding job that was offered."

We were lying together in *Erin's* for'ard cabin, her black hair strewn across a white pillow, her hand resting on my arm, time stolen away from her father's watchful eyes.

I had found work for a few days, washing dishes at a local café. But the wages were minimal, and with no more than a few words of French, they soon tired of me.

I stayed in Saint-Goustan for three weeks. Giselle spent her days working at the same café, nights looking after her mother. The family had exhausted their savings seeking a cure for Colette's cancer. I was now the only hope of saving their home, a small farm that had been in the family for generations.

"We can do it," I told her, "I've been offered that job on Inis Mór. It will take at least six months, and the money will be good."

CHAPTER 1

Gale Force

*"There are more sons lost at sea,
than mothers of a broken heart."*

Anon.

THE WEATHER TOOK a turn for the worse before I lost sight of land. Swells rolling in from the east building rapidly, skies darkening, thunderclouds obscuring the horizon. It did not look good, but it was too late to turn back.

The first gusts struck *Erin* just after two that afternoon. Sudden, angry blasts came out of nowhere, slamming the boat over on her keels end and forcing me to take a reef in her mainsail. But she handled the conditions well, forging ahead confidently, rising to each challenge, cutting through the waters confidently as if born for the task. I pressed on, hoping it would pass, but the seas were rising, the spray thrown back from her bow, soaking me to the skin as we thrust into the heavier swells.

I went below, pulled on wet weather gear, tied a rope around my waist as a safety harness, and went back up on deck. In just a few short hours the scene had changed dramatically. The white clouds of morning had morphed into a melting pot of ominous, purple-black thunderheads, engulfing the sky and melding treacherously with menacing, slate-grey seas.

I fought my way along the deck, the early spattering of rain had turned into a torrent, driving into my face, and blinding me as I struggled for'ard to take in the mainsail. Lorcan had warned that the English Channel was treacherous, but nothing he'd said had prepared me for this.

I lashed the sail to the boom and took stock. The boat was running way too fast, the headsail had to come down. I crawled for'ard again, tied my safety line to the bowsprit stanchion and began unshackling the sail. It was difficult work, waves crashing over the foredeck, threatening to tear me overboard at any moment. It took thirty minutes to replace the sail with a storm jib, a small, heavy sail, with just enough canvas to enable us to claw our way offshore and out to deeper waters.

The ocean was a seething mass of howling winds and rising waves. Picking *Erin* up bodily, raising her higher, higher, and yet higher. The views across the wavetops like some nautical version of Dante's Inferno. Then the descent, plunging down, and down, and down. Down until there was nothing but endless chasms of dark swirling waters all around. No horizon, no division between sea and sky, no trace of land. Just *Erin* and myself, tossed, battered, and completely at the mercy of the elements.

"The land is your enemy in a blow," the old man had said, "head for open water, boy, wait out the gale, it will pass."

I checked the compass and turned further south, running before the wind. The storm jib pulled strongly, giving me some control of my boat.

The rest of that day was nerve-wracking, but as the hours passed, I realized that *Erin* was looking after herself. Slipping gracefully down the watery slopes, rising to meet the breaking seas, heeling over in the harder gusts, then righting herself and pushing ahead with a grace built into her by my grandfather. The wind veered in the late afternoon, we were now running due east, away from the land, out to the safety of the wide Atlantic.

I had enough food and water on board for a week or more, but I was worried. The second-hand radio I had bought in Ireland had never worked, and I knew that Giselle would be waiting for confirmation that I'd arrived back on Inis Mór.

Dinner that night was a half loaf of bread and a tin of tuna, eaten in the cockpit. I couldn't leave the tiller for more than a few minutes at a time, fearful she would round up into the wind and be overwhelmed. By the following morning, I was exhausted. I had no real idea as to my position, and, with my limited navigational skills and overcast sky, no chance of taking reliable bearings. I was relying totally on dead reckoning, which, with my lack of experience, was barely one step up from guesswork.

I battled on throughout the next day, my eyes red raw from peering through salt-washed spray, grabbing a bite to eat whenever I could. Tins of beans, vegetables, or fruit. Huddled in the cockpit, desperately trying to concentrate on the task at hand. The winds around me howling like a thousand demented banshees. The unforgiving waves marching endlessly and forever onwards. My mind exhausted by the constant need to keep the boat stern on to the following waves.

I ran offshore all day and all that night; knowing if I had

enough sea room, I had a better chance of survival. Dawn found me hunched over in the cockpit, sick at heart and disorientated. Dozing off repeatedly, only to be jerked awake by the force of the tiller thumping against my chest. The sky, never-ending shades of black and grey, the ocean swirling around me like a living thing. Me, hanging on to whatever senses I had left, praying that God would look after Giselle if I didn't make it.

That night dragged on and on. Sliding down monstrous waves, rising in almost complete darkness to their peaks, then back down again, and again, and again. By morning I was totally disorientated. I had no idea what time it was or what day it was. "*It's over,*" the voices were starting, "*You're a dreamer, you always were. Let go, stop fighting, everything will be okay.*" But then, in a moment of clarity, I realized I was beginning to hallucinate. I tied the tiller amidships and crawled below, grabbed a cup of hot soup and a handful of biscuits, and climbed back up on deck. The soup helped, but soon my eyelids were drooping again, the biscuits slipping through my fingers, swilling around in the seawater on the cockpit floor…

Gigantic waves towering over me, rearing, and plunging like wild horses, flowing mains of white foam whipping out behind. Their bodies surged beneath the boat only to rise again on the other side. Ethereal voices adding to the confusion, "Consider her side," *they whispered,* "The trip to Brittany wasn't about her, it was all about you. What you wanted, what you needed. You were determined to show her how much you've changed. What a great father you would be. You, you, you. She needs a hero, Conor. A knight in shining armour. Serve the feminine,* *serve your wife…"*

There was a deafening thunderclap directly above and I jolted awake. *Erin* was skittering sideways down the face of a cresting wave. I jerked the tiller over just in time and she righted herself, the wave passing harmlessly beneath her keel. But I knew it couldn't last. Sooner or later, I would fall asleep, run beam onto the seas, and be overwhelmed.

Despite the peril, within minutes, I was dozing again. Giselle's hand reaching out, a voice whispering soft and low… "look to your heart, Conor, come home to your heart…"

And suddenly that roaring sound again, dragging me back to the present. Water poured into the cockpit as I fought with the tiller. *Erin*, driven sideways by cascading waters, was beginning to roll. But miraculously, she regained her footing, turned, and ran down the slope of the next breaking wave to safety.

It dawned on me then, that I had no idea as to where I was, and I reached down into the cabin and flicked on the depths sounder. It was off the chart, too deep to record. There was more than half a mile of water underneath *Erin's* hull, and that simple fact shocked me to my core, and I realised for the first time that I could be dead by morning. Something inside me snapped and leaping to my feet, I began screaming up at the heavens,

"You want to kill me? Then kill me! Kill me! I'm not afraid to die. To hell with you! I'm not afraid of dying! Do it! Do it! For Christ's sake do it!" But then I broke, collapsing back down onto the cockpit seat sobbing like a child, the old man's words coming to me like a dream,

"If you're a lone sailor in a heavy gale, within days *you* will become the problem. Not the weather, not the boat, you." He'd stared at me, his dark green eyes glinting in the half-light of the shed. "Exhaustion will wreck your mind, boy. The only thing you can do when that happens is reduce sail, lash the tiller amidships, and go below. If your vessel is worth her salt, she will look after herself."

Then the voices again, the same ethereal voices I'd heard before I ever came to Inis Mór…

Sometimes there is no logic
As to meaning or to cause
Sometimes the heart must rule the head
Unless we die as slaves
Sometimes at night I lay
Called by Spirit to that shore
And know an Angel's waiting
By the cliffs at Inis Mór
Night waves turning seeking
A half open dark door
Whispered lost memories
From that hard broken shore
Black waves rolling over me
Dark down from the deep
Where lies my purpose
Where will I sleep?

And then I knew what I had to do. Staggering to my feet, I tightened the halyard on the storm sail a notch or two, strapped the tiller firmly amidships and crawled down through the companionway into the cabin. It was chaos below. A mattress from one of the bunks lay on the cabin sole, along with pots and pans and other items escaped from the galley. I ignored it all, slid the hatch shut, closed the doors, collapsed down onto the mattress, and passed out cold.

✧ ✧ ✧

THE DREAMS CAME slowly, hovering in that misty space between consciousness and illusion. I was lying flat on my back in the cabin, staring up at the open companionway. The hatch and the doors wide open. Bright, white lightening flickering against a coal-black sky, thunder rumbling like some dark, primal beast. The boat pitching and tossing. The old man sitting in the cockpit, his collar turned up against wind and rain. His long black greatcoat gathered at the knee. One hand clutching the tiller. His eyes stared straight ahead as if seeking some distant landfall. Is this really happening? I thought. Am I dreaming? I looked around. The cabin was clean and tidy. I went to stand, but he held out a cautionary hand, "Sleep." was all he said. "Go back to sleep, boy."

CHAPTER 2

Return to Inis Mór

*"O Captain! My Captain!
Our fearful trip is done."*

Walt Whitman

I ROSE TO consciousness slowly; weak, weary, and unwilling to relinquish the sanctity of sleep. And as I did, I became aware of the sounds of water rushing alongside the hull. The rolling motion of the boat. Sunshine streaming in through the portholes. The open hatch framing a cloudless blue sky. Was I still dreaming? I sat up. No, it was real. The gale had blown itself out.

Both the sliding hatch and the doors to the cockpit were wide open. I shrugged it off, I'd been half mad with exhaustion when I crawled below. I rose from the bunk, put the kettle on, and staggered up on deck, weak with hunger. The seas were still high, but calmer now, the wind a mere breeze. I unleashed the tiller, turned to take my bearings, and stopped dead. In the distance, perhaps ten or so nautical miles off my port bow, an island rose from the early morning mist. I reached down into the cabin for the binoculars, then trained them on a large stone structure that stood at the highest point of the island. As the building came into focus my heart surged in my chest. It was Dún Árann, the lighthouse that has stood at the highest point of the Island of Inis Mór for over two hundred years.

✧ ✧ ✧

TWO HOURS LATER, as I was closing on the island, a trawler surged out of the harbour and after a few blasts on her foghorn, altered course, towards me. There were people clustered at her bow, waving and shouting, and as they drew closer, I recognized Lorcan, Mary, and the postmaster, Tim. The trawler passed to starboard then swung around and approached *Erin* from her stern.

"Wind and tide are against you, Conor." The skipper was bellowing from the wheelhouse, "We'll be towing you from here." Then, "Go aboard, Michael, he's done in. Get a rope around that Samson post."

Lorcan was waving, Mary huddled at his side. I just stared back, too weak to respond. Michael came on board, dropped the storm sail, and secured the tow line, and a few minutes later we entered the harbour. He'd offered to steer, but I'd refused. We'd come this far together; we'd finish the trip as one. Once the water began to shallow, I called out,

"Let go the towline, Michael," and then a moment later, "Let go the anchor." As the chain rattled down over the bow, I collapsed back down on the cockpit seat. It was over at last. I was home.

✧ ✧ ✧

MICHAEL ROWED ME ashore in the trawler's dinghy. A small

crowd had gathered, and after being hugged by Mary, every man and woman on the quayside embraced me. Some muttering words in Irish that I took to be a welcome. I was overwhelmed by emotion and found myself close to tears at times. Lorcan told me later that the words spoken had been traditional blessings for those thought lost at sea. For every family on Inis Mór has lost a son, a daughter, or a friend to the Atlantic Ocean.

✧ ✧ ✧

"Jaysus, Conor, we had you dead and gone!" We were walking home to the Reardon's cottage. Mary's arm through mine. Lorcan chiding me about the trip.

"Did you not check the forecast?"

"I did," I told him, "The weather looked fine the day I set out."

"Well, like I told you, never trust the Channel; and you need to be getting *Erin* up into the shed before too long, she'll not survive the winter in the harbour."

"Will you leave him be for God's sake," Mary snapped, "do you not see he's exhausted?" She was hugging my arm tightly, as if afraid to let go of me. "Your wife knows you're home safe, Conor. As soon as they sighted *Erin* one of the fishermen ran up here to tell us. I called her straight away. She was worried sick, the poor girl. She hadn't told Tristan, she hadn't the heart. God almighty, you gave us a terrible fright!"

"Well, it's over now." Lorcan was opening the cottage door, "You're back, that's all that matters. You know your grandfather was lost from that same boat. It brought it all back for Mary."

I called Giselle as soon as we got in, "It wasn't too bad," I told her; "Once the gale started, I ran offshore. She's a good little boat, Giselle, you shouldn't have worried."

"Don't make light of it, Conor," she was in tears. "You were missing for a week. I was worried sick. Tristan was just starting to trust you."

"I was out there for three days," I said, "maybe four, don't make it any worse than it was."

"You were gone for a week, Conor, eight days to be exact. It was reckless. You don't have the experience, you know that."

✧ ✧ ✧

AFTER TALKING WITH Giselle, I soaked in the bath for an hour. Lorcan returned several times to add buckets of scalding water and clumps of dried seaweed to the tub. The aches, pains, and terrors of the voyage, gradually loosening their grip in the steam-filled room.

When I turned up in the kitchen Mary had a meal prepared, and we sat around the table eating, Lorcan doing most of the talking.

"So, what are your plans, or is it too soon to ask?" He was assessing me from behind his glasses. "You're famous now, but for all the wrong reasons. It was all over the news in Galway. They have you labeled an Australian Yachtsman; it'll take a while to live that one down. They would have picked up the story from the radio station here, no doubt."

"Does that doctor still want me to fix his boat?" I asked.

"Dr. Finlayson? I'd imagine so. Sure he was mad keen

when we met him last time,"

"Can we contact him?"

"We can of course, he gave me his card, it would be around here somewhere. But that boat is in ruins, Conor. I was up there with Michael Greely, he's one of the fishermen. I didn't go up above, I'm too old to be climbing ladders, but Greely did. He said she'll need a total rebuild and she's twice the size of *Erin*. It would cost a small fortune."

"So why not buy a new boat?" I said, "Does he have that kind of money?"

"That and more. He's one of the richest men in Ireland. Owns a chain of hotels around the world I'm told. He hasn't practiced medicine for years. Just likes the title I suppose."

"We'd have to work out how much it would cost," I said. "He'd want a quote I'd imagine."

"No, impossible. You couldn't quote on a job like that. You'd give him a labor cost, weekly or monthly. Some estimates as to time, although that won't be easy. He supplies everything after that. Materials, timber, fittings, paint, anything that's needed. There's no other way it could be done."

"Do you think we can do it?" I asked.

"Well, you'd need the right men, of course. There's no one on the island building boats just now, so you'd need to get a couple of men over from Galway." He was nodding, agreeing with himself. "I'll be there whenever I can, I helped your grandfather with *Erin* many a time."

"Don't be putting yourself forward as a boatbuilder, Lorcan Reardon." Mary came in, "You're a schoolteacher and a retired one at that. You haven't lifted a hammer in forty years."

"I lay no claims as to being a boatbuilder, Mary. I said I'd be there to help and help I will."

"Go off to bed now, Conor, you look exhausted." Mary was shaking her head." Sure, you're back five minutes and he has you building boats again. Go off to bed now and stay there. We'll talk again in the morning."

CHAPTER 3

Hope

I OPENED MY eyes reluctantly the following day, stirred from sleep by a gentle tapping on the bedroom door.

"Are you there, Conor?" Mary's voice, soft and hesitant, "It's after nine."

The shower enveloped me like a blessing. Fresh hot water streaming down my face and shoulders. Sunlight pouring in through pebbled glass. A pristine bar of pure white soap. Steam swirling in the air. A razor cutting through days of stubble. A clean, white towel rubbed hard against my skin.

I arrived in the kitchen a few minutes later, the smell of bacon and toast reminding me of just how hungry I was.

"Jaysus, Conor, you look half-starved!" Lorcan was pulling on an overcoat by the front door.

"I didn't eat much on the boat," I told him, "It was pretty wild out there."

"I'm off to see Fergal O'Shea about having *Erin* slipped. That's a private mooring you're on so we need to have it done before too long." He slid a card across the table, "That's the doctor's card there now, give him a call," I picked it up.

OMEGAN EXON INC.

INTERNATIONAL GOLF RESORTS

NEW YORK – DUBAI – LONDON

WWW.OMEGANEXONINC.IE.

I turned the card over. Scribbled on the back, in a barely legible scrawl, a phone number.

"There you go, Conor," Mary was by the table with a plate of food, "and there's coffee and toast on the way."

✧ ✧ ✧

As soon as breakfast was over, I walked down to the quay. *Erin* was bobbing to a mooring out in the middle of the harbour.

"You can't leave her there for too long," the harbour master appeared alongside. A black patch over one eye, a grizzled grey beard that reached to his greatcoat, an old seaman's cap pulled low, "That mooring belongs to one of the trawlers. She's over in Galway having her engines done, so you'll be right for a week or so. I'll let Lorcan know when she's due back in."

I thanked him, borrowed a dinghy, and rowed out to *Erin*. She was lying there peacefully, like a swan on a lake. I climbed on board and went down the hatchway. It was chaos below. A mattress from one of the bunks lay on the cabin sole covered with cans of tinned fruit, packets of pasta, tea bags, and various items escaped from the cupboards.

I spent the next few hours tidying up. Getting everything back in its place. Sorting out the mess in the for'ard cabin. Cleaning the galley area and bagging all the clothing that needed washing.

But around two pm the exhaustion crept back in, so I

closed *Erin* up, went ashore, rode my bike home to my cottage, and fell into bed.

✧   ✧   ✧

Just after five that evening I was awakened by a loud banging on the front door and going below I found Lorcan standing there holding a wicker basket.

"Were you sleeping?" he pushed through the door sideways, "Mary's convinced you're on your last legs with hunger," he didn't wait for an answer, "Where can I leave this?" I followed him through into the kitchen, "There's ham, eggs, sausage, and beans. Did you call Dr. Finlayson?"

"No, I have to charge my phone. I'll call him in the morning,"

"Good. And make sure you tell him the boat's in bad shape. He'll need to come over and see for himself."

"I'll tell him," I said, "but I'm pretty sure he's aware of that."

CHAPTER 4

Bankruptcy

I WOKE UP late the following morning. Heavy grey clouds scudding across a darkened horizon, the thunder rumbling in the distance, reminding me that winter was almost upon us.

I pulled on a dressing gown, went below, lit a fire, made coffee, then dialed Patrick Finlayson's number. The message, in his own voice, was short and to the point, "Leave your name and number after the tone. I'll get back to you."

"Patrick, this is Conor O'Rourke, from Inis Mór. We met a few months back. I'm the guy who rebuilt *Erin*. I'm back on Inis Mór. Call me when you can." I left my number.

I tried three times that day, and a dozen times in the days that followed. All with the same result, silence.

"He'd be a busy man, Conor." Lorcan assured me, "Don't worry your head about Patrick, he'll be back to you before the week's out, you'll see,"

But that didn't happen, so I sent an email. No response. That was when I began to worry.

"What do you know about him?" Lorcan had invited me for dinner, "Does he live in Galway?"

"No idea. His father had his practice there. A little place in Salt Hill. I was there once or twice myself, but that was donkeys years ago,"

"So, you don't know much about him?"

"Patrick? No, not much. He's a bit of a highflyer. In the newspapers from time to time. Business stuff, you know. Last I heard he was opening some big hotel in London."

When I got home, I fired up my laptop and checked out the website. It was impressive. Images of golf resorts in different countries. Hollywood celebrities shaking hands with Sheiks in Saudi Arabia, minor British royals mingling with famous golfers in the USA, but no phone numbers. I found the contact page and sent off a message.

> *Private and Confidential. Please relay this to Dr. Patrick Finlayson.*
>
> *Hi Patrick. Conor O'Rourke here. We met a few months ago on Inis Mór. You asked me to refit your boat, The Maid of Aran. I'm back on the island now and looking forward to talking to you about the project. Please call me any time. Conor.*

I included my phone number, said a prayer, and pressed send.

✧ ✧ ✧

THE FOLLOWING DAYS were difficult. Waiting for a response. Calling his number twice a day, morning, and evening. Not leaving messages now in case I was overdoing things. Worrying about Giselle.

By the end of the week, I was totally confused. Not able to take charge of the situation, totally dependent on some other human being. Unable to make decisions of my own or move ahead. Angry with Finlayson one minute, making excuses for him the next.

The following Monday morning, when I checked my emails. There was a message from a company calling itself Roberts, Cahill, & Slater; advising me that Omegan Exon Inc. had entered receivership and if they owed me money, or if I was I indebted to them in any way, I should fill in the attached forms and remit them as early as possible.

I stared at the email, sick to my stomach. The company was bankrupt. I made coffee, took a mug out to my perch at the back of the cottage, and sat there staring out over the ocean.

The day was overcast, the seas calm, waves breaking softly in the cove below, my mind racing.

Bankruptcy, it pulls you apart. It devours you. All your time, all your energy. I knew how it felt, I'd just barely missed it myself. This explains the silence. I'd be the least of his worries.

I don't know how long I sat there churning over recent events. The promises I'd made to Giselle. Her trusting face. Her doubts. The tentative smiles. Wanting to believe me.

"Christ!" I should have waited until the job was secure before making all the promises. The same mistake, over and over again. Persuading her to see things my way. Talk, talk, talk. Promises, promises. Promises that always seemed to fall apart somehow.

But then another thought. Maybe I could find a job on the island. Like what? I don't know, but there must be something. Tourism, washing dishes, anything.

I pulled on my leather jacket and rode down to Lorcan's place. Mary was just arriving home on her bicycle.

"Dr. Finlayson's broke," I told her, "Or at least his company's bankrupt."

"Of God," a hand to her cheek, "So the boat job's gone?"

"It looks like that. I can't contact him."

"What will you do, Conor?"

"I'm not sure. Try to find a job on the island I guess,"

"Doing what?" But then she paused, "wait, hold on now, wasn't I talking to Fiona O'Shea at church last week. She owns the hotel over on the quay. She had two Dublin men working as barmen there. Well, the next thing you know the Guardia arrives over from Galway and arrests the both of them. They were hiding out here it seems. Go over there now and talk to her, she may have something for you."

I headed down to the quayside. The hotel stood on the front street, facing out across the harbour. A two-story building with a steeply gabled slate roof, bay windows, and a small garden out front.

✧ ✧ ✧

"Yes, I know who you are." We were standing in the bar by a large open fire. She was a tall, thin woman, dressed in blue jeans, a white blouse, navy-blue cardigan and Reebok sports shoes, her hair tied back in a ponytail, "You're Con Rua O'Rourke's boy, back from Australia. Mary's a friend of mine. Sure, she was in bits here last week when they thought you lost from that old boat of yours," she was sizing me up, a quizzical look on her face, "And you're a boatbuilder?"

"I rebuilt my father's boat," I told her, "Over in the shed there. Before that, I was in advertising in Australia."

"Look," she gestured, "I had this place rented out for years and it was not looked after right. But we've most of the work done already."

"Mary thought you might need a barman?"

"We did, but we have a man across from Galway two days ago, and he's shaping up well. We'll need another for the Christmas, we have the place booked out. Did you ever work behind a bar?"

"No, but I spent a lot of time in front of bars, before I stopped drinking that is."

"Mary mentioned you were teetotal. Are you a Pioneer or something?"

"No, nothing like that. I had to stop. It got the best of me, but I'm fine now."

"Did Mary tell you I'm a member of Alcoholics Anonymous?"

"No, she didn't mention that."

"No, she wouldn't have, that was told to her in confidence," she was staring at me, "Is there something you need to tell me?"

"Well, I was in AA in Australia for a while,"

"Then why not say?"

"I haven't had a drink in over two years," I told her.

"Did you have a sponsor?"

"Yes, she helped me a lot."

"Does she know where you are now?"

"No, we lost contact when I came over here."

"You mean you lost contact; right?"

"Yes, I haven't contacted her since I left Sydney."

"Look, I'll be straight with you, Conor. I had a bar manager here a few years back. I met him in the rehab where I got sober. Well, he turned up here on Inis Mór six months after, begging me to give him the start. He'd worked for some of the best hotels in Dublin and he had good references."

"And you took him on?"

"Yes, more fool me. I told him there were AA meetings on the island, but he said he was concerned for his anonymity. Said if it ever got out that he was an alcoholic, he'd never again get a decent job in Ireland. I should have known better, but I wasn't sober long myself at the time."

"So, it didn't work out."

"No, it was a disaster. The first few weeks were fine, and I'm convinced to this day he was sober that time. But takings began to fall the second month. One of the staff warned me there was something going on, but I didn't believe her. I watched him of course, but he never set a foot wrong. He'd hold up a glass of mineral water behind the bar, like a joke you know, 'Fresh water is good for the soul' he'd tell them. 'Although fish do pee in it,' he'd say. They all thought he was a great craic altogether," her eyes narrowed. "It was only after I caught him with his hand in the till and fired him that we cleaned out his room. There were seventy-three empty whiskey bottles up there in the wardrobe! Johny Walker, Jamesons, Glenfiddich, Jim Beam, you name it."

"You're trying to tell me something?"

"Conor, I'll not be responsible for you picking up a drink. I'll not put you behind a bar only to see you fail. Sure, it would break Mary's heart. She told me about your wife and child.

That's a lot of stress, and you know what can happen if we're stressed for too long. If you're a recovering alcoholic wanting to work in a pub, you need to get yourself back into the rooms." She paused, "Now, it's not my business to be telling you what you should or shouldn't be doing. But there's a meeting over in the hall tonight. It's there every Wednesday. You should come along and meet some of the members. You can decide then if it's for you or not."

"I will," I said, "What time?"

"Eight o'clock and call your sponsor. They tend to worry when their pigeons fly away like that," a smile crossed her face. "Look, our dishwasher goes off on holiday in two weeks, back home to Belfast. It's only part-time, but it's something. And we might want to try you out as a barman closer to Christmas."

"What about the money side of things?"

"How does twenty euro an hour sound?" Mary had warned me she was tough.

"Twenty-five would be better," I told her.

"Will we settle on twenty-two so?"

"Twenty-two is fine. When do I start?"

"Two weeks from today, unless you find something better," her handshake was as firm as any man. "And tell Mary I was asking after her."

✧ ✧ ✧

AFTER LEAVING THE hotel I stopped off at the shed, and stepping through the door I was surprised to find Lorcan sitting in one of the armchairs.

"Mary said I might find you here," he stood up, "It's bad

news about Patrick."

"Yes, I was counting on that job."

"Well, you know what they say, the quicker they rise, the harder they fall."

"Sure," I said, "I know something about that myself,"

"So, how did you go with Fiona O'Shea, was she over there?"

"Yes, she offered me a casual job for a couple of weeks, that's all she has. And there may be something for a few weeks over Christmas,"

"Well, that's about all you can hope for on the island, m'boy. And then there'll be no tourists at all after the Christmas till May or June."

"There's nothing else on the island?"

"No, nothing at all. There's tourism and fishing, that's about it. We lose most of our young people each year. They go off to Galway or Dublin. And then a lot of them head off overseas from there."

After he left, I sat in the armchair, depression stirring like a cancer stirring in the darker recesses of my mind. Where to from here? I'd have to tell Giselle. I can't bring her to Inis Mór without a job. I'd painted such a rosy picture. You're good at that, I thought, you were always good at conning people, even better when you were drinking. Drinking. Christ! A drink would help right now. Just a few. Just to give me a break. Then I'd stop. Who would know? The thought shook me, and I realized I was on dangerous ground.

I stood up and looked around. I'd failed to tidy the shed before leaving for Brittany and the place was a mess. I turned the radio on full blast, grabbed a broom, and went at it. Music blaring, dust flying, working like a madman, running from the demons.

CHAPTER 5

Meetings

I ARRIVED AT the meeting hall a little before eight. A dim glow coming through the open doors. A circle of chairs. A few shadowy figures wrapped in coats and anoraks. Someone sitting behind an old wooden desk.

"Good evening."

I turned. A tall figure, in a long black overcoat, was standing in the shadows just inside the doorway. He looked to be about the same age as myself, and as he reached out a hand, I realised it was the priest.

"Hi," I was taken aback, "You're off the drink?"

I regretted the words as soon as they were out of my mouth.

"I am the greeter here tonight," he gripped my hand, "Do I know you?"

"We met at Madge O'Neil's wake," I told him, "I'm Conor O'Rourke."

"Of course you are!" a lop-sided grin, "And you've come to the right place, Conor," he leaned forwards, a whiff of alcohol, tainted by breath freshener, "Sure the drink will pull a man down quicker than the divil himself!"

I reclaimed my hand and found a seat. There were a dozen or so people present, five women, the rest men. No sign of

Fiona O'Shea. I looked around. It was different to the meetings I'd been to in Australia. Set in a circle that expanded as each new person joined the group.

The chairperson opened the meeting at eight and told us her name was Aisleen. Then she announced that it was an 11th Step meeting, before inviting those present to identify with their first names and sobriety dates.

"My name's Moira, I'm an alcoholic." The first to identify was a woman was in her mid-thirties; "And I'm sober now these past three months,"

"Well done,"

"Good woman,"

"Fine girl you are, Moira."

Affirming comments were offered by most of the group.

"My name's Joe," he was an older man in a heavy overcoat and an Americanized Irish accent, "I'm an alcoholic, and I'm sober forty-nine years."

I was sixth in line, "My name's Conor," I was surprised how nervous I was, "I'm sober a couple of years, but I haven't been to a meeting for a while."

"Welcome back, Conor."

"You're welcome here, Conor."

"You're in the right room, Conor, keep coming back."

Simple and ritualistic as they were, the words touched me, making me realize how much I'd missed the fellowship.

Once everyone had identified, the chairwoman told us her name was Aisleen and that she was sober for six years.

"Now, tonight we're taking a look at the eleventh step. Joe here is home from the USA visiting family, and I've asked him to be our guest speaker for the first five or ten minutes."

Joe nodded to her. "Thank you, Aisleen. My name's Joe, I'm an alcoholic," he looked around, "I joined AA in Boston, Massachusetts, at the age of thirty-three. I was a construction worker who hadn't worked in years. I'd lost my wife and children through the drink. I was homeless, helpless, and hopeless. Dossing in a laneway called La Grange Street, the worst area in what was then known as the Combat Zone. Living rough with winos, deadbeats, and junkies," he shook his head, "I was a sorry case altogether. But we're not here for a drinking story. We're here to take a look at this step." He looked around the circle. "This is the step that set me free and introduced me to the meaning and purpose of my life. And just to be clear, this step does not belong to Alcoholics Anonymous, it belongs to the world. The guy who wrote the program, Bill Wilson, was simply rephrasing an age-old truth that had been known and understood for millennia; that there is a meaning and a purpose to every human life."

As he spoke, I realised that this was exactly the same as the old man's teachings.

"Do you see what this step is suggesting? We're to use prayer and meditation to seek out God's will for us. It's about discovering what our purpose is in life. This is an action step, it is not passive. It's about seeking out the meaning of our existence. It's about waking up. Carpe Diem! It's about seizing the day!" He paused, realising that everyone in the room was staring at him. "Look, I'm sorry. I get carried away at times," he smiled, and the smile took twenty years off his face, "You see, this step created a whole new life for me. I went from being a semi-literate, low-life, skid row bum, to a successful businessman with a family that now includes children, grandchildren, and great-grandchildren." He paused and glanced across at the chairwoman, "Time's about up?"

"How does the group feel," Aisling looked around, "do we want Joe to continue, or should I call on others to share?"

"Can I ask him a question?" a woman asked.

"Is the group all right with that?" Aisling looked around the circle. "Give me a show of hands," it was unanimous.

"I'm Moira, Joe. So, should I be working on this step now?"

"You're sober for three months, right?"

"Yes, just over three months,"

"Then the answer's no, Moira. Don't worry about the eleventh step just yet. Work the program and get yourself right first."

"Could I ask what you do, Joe?" A thick-set guy with craggy features was leaning forward in his chair, "For a living I mean."

"I'm an author, books, screenplays, movies, that's my calling, and I found it through this step."

"Joe, I'm a member of the clergy," the priest was leaning forward, his glassy eyes fixed on Joe, "and I've been coming here for the past two years, but I've never had more than a few day's sobriety."

"And your name,"

"Father Aiden O'Grady.'

"Well, no offense, Aiden, but there are no priests or vicars in these rooms; same as there are no kings or presidents. Do you have a sponsor?"

"No, but like I said, I'm a member of the clergy, so I already have a good grasp on spiritual matters."

"Aiden," Joe was still smiling, "I'll be blunt with you, for without the truth you may never get sober at all. If you have such a good grasp of spiritual matters, how come the other spirit, the spirit of ethyl alcohol, is still so important to you that you can't go without it for more than a few days at a time? Now, you don't have to answer that just yet. Maybe just think about it for a while."

"What if you're sober for a while and nothing's working out?" I asked.

"Your name's Conor, right?" he asked.

"Yes."

"You mentioned you've been away from the fellowship?"

"Yes."

"How long since your last drink?"

"About two years."

"And have you helped another alcoholic in that time?"

"No, I've been busy trying to get my life back together. I'm trying to find work so that my wife and son can join me here."

"Have you ever sponsored anyone?"

"No."

"Conor, how can you expect the power to run through you if you're not prepared to pass it on?" He smiled, "Should we talk after the meeting?"

"I'd appreciate that," I told him.

✧ ✧ ✧

THE MEETING WOUND up at eight, with coffee and cake after. Joe was visiting from Boston. At eighty-two, diagnosed with terminal cancer, he was here to say goodbye to a few old friends and relations.

"You have an Australian accent."

"I was born in Galway, but my father was an islander. He was killed in a car crash in Dublin. We moved to Australia when I was eight."

"And you've drifted away from the meetings?"

"Yes, I didn't know there were meetings on the island."

"And your life's in tatters again?"

"Yes. Nothing's working out. I've nearly convinced my wife to come over here and join me, but the job I was offered fell through and I'm afraid to tell her."

"And how's the head?"

"Not good. I've been offered a job in a pub, but it's just for a week or two, and that's not going to change anything. It all seems so bloody hopeless. I've been thinking about getting back on the anti-depressants."

"You're on shaky ground, Conor. Self-prescribed drugs can be the first step towards picking up a drink for an alcoholic."

"So, what do I do?"

"You help another alcoholic."

"And what if they are not interested?"

"That's not your responsibility. Your only responsibility is to offer that help. The result is up to the Higher Power."

We talked for hours and it was midnight before I got home. The fire was still flickering in the grate. I made a hot drink and sat there for a while, mulling over the day, before climbing the stairs to bed.

CHAPTER 6

Father Aiden

IT WAS AFTER nine when I arrived at the boatshed the next day. One of the big doors was open but walking through, the shed appeared to be empty. I looked around, a fire was burning in the hearth, empty Guinness bottles on the ground.

I climbed *Erin's* ladder, and as I stepped down into the cabin, I was greeted by a smell of alcohol and a loud groan.

"Oooh, God, who's that?" The voice came from the for'ard cabin and as I moved closer the priest's head appeared from beneath a paint-spattered drop sheet, "Where am I?"

"You're in my boat," I told him, "How did you get up here?"

"No idea," he raised himself up on an elbow, "Is there a drink in the house? I have a terrible head on me."

"Drink that," I said, handing him the tea.

"Is there nothing stronger?"

"Are you okay to get back down?"

"I'll try," he said.

I went below and moments later he was in the cockpit, fumbling with the ladder.

"Careful," I called out, "Get a good grip on that ladder."

He made it down safely then slumped in an armchair by the fire. He looked terrible, face grey, eyes bloodshot, hair like a haystack. All accompanied by the bitter stench of stale Guinness.

"It's fierce cold up there!" he had his arms wrapped around himself, leaning in towards the fire.

"How did you get up there?" I asked.

"God alone would know that," he had both hands held out to the rising flames, "I've woke in stranger places."

"You could have broken your neck going up that ladder," I told him.

"God looks after drunks, brown dogs, and little children," he smiled at me sideways, "That's what the Bishop of Galway told me before sending me over here for a penance." He was looking around the shed, "Do you not have a drop of something, Conor? Anything at all, I'm in desperate need of a drink."

"There's nothing here, mate," I told him, "And if there was, I wouldn't give it to you."

"Oh God almighty, don't they say there's nothing worse than a recovered alcoholic."

"Whoever *they* are," I told him, "would probably change their minds after looking at you."

"Could you loan me a few euros then, just enough to get me started for the day?"

"No. No money. But what I will do, I'll be your sponsor. If you want to stop drinking that is."

"I have to stop drinking." He looked up at me, "Do you not see? I'm about to be defrocked. I've been told that by the bishop himself."

"But do you want to stop drinking?"

"I have to. I have no choice."

"But do you want to?"

"For God's sake, Conor, I have no choice!"

"Okay," I told him, "I'll be your sponsor."

"And what would that look like?"

"Well, whatever you've been doing hasn't worked, so we'll be trying something different."

"You're right about that, I'd need something different," he pondered for a few moments longer, "When do we start?"

"We start right now. Do not take a drink of alcohol for the next twenty-four hours; understood? Just twenty-four hours, one day. You think you can do that?"

"Sure anyone can do that. It's tomorrow or the next day I'd be worried about."

"Keep it in the day," I told him, "Just the next twenty-four hours; okay? When you wake up in the morning, the same again, understand. One day at a time. And be at the meeting next Wednesday, we'll talk again then."

We shook hands and he left. I watched him walk off up the road, stumbling and weaving like his knees were on backward.

◆ ◆ ◆

I WAS FITTING a new aerial on the two-way radio in *Erin's* cabin an hour later when my mobile shrilled below on the bench. I hurried down but missed the call. I rang back.

"Patrick Finlayson."

"Patrick!" I was thrown, "It's Conor O'Rourke here, from Inis Mór."

"Conor! How are you? I arrived back from the States last night and got your message. How are things on the island?"

"Fine, but I heard things have gone bad for you."

"Meaning?"

"The bankruptcy, I got a message from the receivers,"

"Forgive me, Conor, but I have no idea at all as to what you're talking about. Who's bankrupt?"

"Your business, Omegan Exon…"

There was a burst of laughter from the other end.

"Exon? No, I have no connection at all with Exon, what gave you that idea?"

"The card. The business card you left; you wrote your home number on the back."

"Oh, I see. No, Exon did approach us months ago looking for investors. That must have been a card one of their people gave me at the time. But no, I have no connection with them at all."

"So, everything's okay?"

"You mean my company? Yes, of course. We're sound, never better."

"And *The Maid of Aran*, do you still want her refitted?"

"I do of course. As I told you, it's been a dream of mine for years. Look, I'm on another call right now, but I'll be over on the ferry first thing in the morning, we can talk then."

✧   ✧   ✧

AFTER HE'D HUNG up, I stood there stunned. Then I ran across to the Reardon's cottage and burst in the door. Lorcan was sitting at the table, a bowl of soup in front of him.

"Patrick Finlayson just called," I told him, "He's not bankrupt, that was some other company."

"Whoa! Slow down, Conor, slow down," he held up a hand, "Dr. Finlayson called?"

"Is the Doctor back?" Mary was standing in the doorway, a book in one hand.

"Yes, he just called. I had it all wrong, the card he left wasn't his. He's not bankrupt, he's fine. We're back in business."

"Did you mention the state of the boat?" Lorcan was frowning.

"No, I couldn't. I haven't been up there yet,"

"Well don't get too excited. As I said, she's in bad shape,"

"Will you stop, Lorcan," Mary was shaking her head, "Could you not say something positive for once in your life?"

"I don't want Conor getting his hopes up, Mary. That boat's in ruins, and while that might not be a positive thing to say, it is the truth."

"It's the truth according to a fisherman. Michael Greely's not a boatbuilder, my love."

"True, true, I'll not argue that," Lorcan held up his hands, "We'll take a look tomorrow, so."

"You should stay with us tonight," Mary was still mothering me, "Your room's made up for you and you can have dinner with us here this evening. Then you'll be ready to meet the doctor in the morning."

CHAPTER 7

The Deal

I OPENED MY eyes reluctantly the next day, stirred from sleep by a gentle tapping on the bedroom door.

"It's after eight, Conor. Dr. Finlayson will be arriving soon."

Lorcan was standing in the kitchen as I arrived, a cup of tea in hand, Mary peering out the window.

"The ferry's offshore there now, so you'll not have time for breakfast," she was wiping her hands on an apron. "I tapped on your door at seven but didn't have the heart to wake you. Take yourselves off to the café. The doctor will need something to no doubt." She handed me a mug of tea. "That's the best I can do for the moment."

✧ ✧ ✧

BY THE TIME we arrived on the quayside, Patrick Finlayson was striding down the gangplank carrying an overnight bag.

"Conor!" We shook hands, "You're a sight for sore eyes."

"You too," I told him, "Welcome back to Inis Mór, Patrick."

"How was the trip to France?"

"Fine," I told him, "*Erin's* a good little sea boat."

He shook hands with Lorcan, "I'm booked in at the Pier House Hotel; will you join me for breakfast?"

The hotel was a short walk to the end of the quay, and once he'd checked in and we'd ordered breakfast, the conversation turned to his boat.

"Did you have a chance to look at her?" he asked.

"No, I haven't been up there yet."

"Well, I'm told she's in bad shape, I just hope we can set her right."

"She's all of that, Patrick," Lorcan was shaking his head, "I was up there with Michael Greely. She's a long way from what she once was."

"But you think you can bring her back?"

"*Erin* was pretty much a wreck too," I told him, "I'll need to have a look at her, but if her basic structure is sound, there's no reason why we can't set her right."

"Good man," he said, "Come on now lads, we'll head up there and see what can be done."

As we set off up the road, he told us of his hopes for the boat.

"She's a Bad Mór, the biggest of the Galway Hookers. I promised my da I'd get her back in the water, but it's more than that. Some of my happiest memories are of sailing with my father. Mostly to the islands here, but he took us on other trips too. We were over to Liverpool a few times, his brother worked there for years, and to France on one occasion. He was a great doctor, but his real passion was sailing. He had her in the Fastnet race twice. Not so much to win now, more for the craic. But after reading Chichester's book about sailing around the world, he became obsessed with the idea. Then he fell ill, cancer of all things. He was just getting over that when the strokes hit him, two the same year. After that, he was just a shadow of a man. Seeing your own father like that, you know, it had a big effect on me." He paused, "He left me a note in the will. I could hardly read the handwriting. He told me to take her back to her original name. You see, he changed her name after buying her."

"What was her original name?"

"*Anam Cara*, it's Irish for: a friend of my soul. I still have the old nameplate on the wall of my office in Galway. I'll bring it across next time I'm over. The fishermen believe if you change a boat's name you must leave the original name on board to avoid bad luck. He didn't do that, and he blamed himself for all the bad luck that followed."

"So how did she end up here on Inis Mór?" I asked.

"Sheer misfortune. He sailed her over here that last time for the blessing of the fleet. There was a bit of a blow on that day, and she was damaged as she came alongside the jetty. Stove in a few of her planks. They managed to pull her up out of the water before she sank, then they built a cradle around her on the quay and hauled her up to the Reagan's place."

"How long has she been up there?" I asked.

"Fourteen years, Da had carpenters over from Galway to build the cradle, then she was dragged up the road there to Reagan's barn. She's been there ever since. The widow has the place sold now to a man from Inis Oírr, and he wants the boat gone."

✧ ✧ ✧

The widow Reagan was waiting by the gate as we arrived. A tall, angular woman, bent over slightly with age, completely dressed in black. A pair of wire-rimmed glasses perched on a prominent nose. Snow white hair tied in a tight bun at the back of her head. An old-fashioned sweeping broom held in both hands.

The cottage was a typical Aran dwelling, with whitewashed walls, a thatch roof, a stone wall surrounding the yard, rows of potatoes dug in a field alongside, a horse grazing nearby.

"Good morning, Gráinne, it's a pleasure to see you."

"And you too, Doctor. You're looking well."

"And you're looking younger every time I lay eyes on you. If I wasn't a married man, I'd have brought flowers."

"Ah, away with you now, Doctor, sure I'm on my last legs as well you know," her eyes were bright as she looked me over. "So, who do we have here with us now?"

"This is Conor. He's Con Rua O'Rourke boy, the seanachaí."

"Oh, of course he is," she had a hand to her mouth, "Sure you're the living image of him, are you not? I heard you were back home on the island. Tim the postman told me you were down there by the quay rebuilding that old boat of your da's. Well, God bless you, Conor, and welcome home." She turned back to Patrick. "Would you have time for the tea, Doctor? I have some lovely fresh soda bread there now, just made."

"Thank you, Gráinne, but we're only just after eating. I've brought Conor up to take a look at the boat. She's been out of the water too long and I promised my da I'd have her fixed."

"Ah, he was a good man was your da. Sure, he spent half his life on the islands. But wait now and I'll fetch the keys."

✧ ✧ ✧

As the barn doors swung open, I was taken aback. A much larger boat than *Erin* stood there, silent and stoic in the gloom, as if awaiting news of her fate. Abandoned boats carry an aura. There's a sorrow about them, a palpable hurt that they could be treated this way. A brooding anger expressed in sullen silence; a female deserted after giving all she had.

"Forgive me, Doctor," Gráinne had her hands clasped together as if in prayer. "There was no way I could look after her right after Donnacha passed. The best I could do was to lock her up and keep her safe from the weather. Then you had the chickens and mice; I don't know what else."

"She's fine, Gráinne. You couldn't have done more. I'll be eternally grateful to you."

She hurried off, the troublesome part of her morning done, leaving us all staring at the boat. No one spoke for what seemed like an age.

"She's in bad shape," the doctor offered at last, "worse than I thought."

She was, and I wondered how she'd made it ashore at all. Her rudder swung drunkenly from one bronze fastening, like a broken leg. Planks at her bow were stove in. Her brass portholes green with mold, some of the glass shattered. The paint on her hull was in tatters, dust laden spider webs hanging like shrouds from her guardrails. While higher up on the coach roof, a red and black rooster observed us suspiciously with an arrogant tilt of his head. The overall impression was of a battered old wreck, dragged up in disgrace from the ocean floor.

A ladder stood at the aft end, and I climbed carefully, wondering just how far gone she was. The cockpit was strewn with rubbish, clumps of straw, feathers, broken eggshells, and droppings scattered everywhere. It was clear that chickens had been roosting there for years.

I forced open the main hatch, eased myself down into the boat, and stood there looking around. It was huge down there, and it was a disaster. A chart table to the right, a galley to the left, a dirty cooking stove covered in bird droppings. Beyond that, the main cabin, was half buried in rubbish. Crumpled canvas sails lay on the bunks stiff and green with mold, while tattered remnants of nautical charts lay in shreds around them. Rusting tin cans, some with labels, some without, lay scattered on the cabin floor. Interspersed with oilskins, molding yellow life jackets, rotting woolen sweaters, a captain's peaked cap, and several enameled tin mugs. The diffused light, entering through grimy portholes, adding an ethereal touch to a chaotic scene. All in all, a degraded time capsule of the day they'd dragged her up out of the water. And I knew at once that I was in trouble.

Patrick came down next, followed several minutes later by Lorcan. There was another long, drawn-out silence. When the doctor finally spoke, it was clear he was shaken.

"Jesus," he said, "I had no idea she was this far gone. I haven't been aboard her since the day she left Galway." He sat down on the starboard bunk, his eyes roaming around the interior. "We may have to rethink this whole thing."

"*Erin* was as bad." I told him, "Save for the damage at the bow and a bit of rot here and there, I'd say *Erin* was as bad."

"I'd love to believe that," he was shaking his head, "It's just a shock, seeing her like this. She was like a second home to me."

"Did you not have anyone look her over since?" Lorcan sat down on the port side bunk, still breathing heavily from the ladder.

"My father had a report from the men he sent over to build the cradle. They said they thought she could be put right. But they weren't boatbuilders, and she would have looked a lot better fourteen years ago no doubt," he glanced around, "Come on lads, I've seen enough."

As they climbed back up the ladder, I went through into the for'ard section of the boat. There was a toilet on one side, a wet weather gear closet on the other. Then a door in a bulkhead leading to a good-sized private cabin that was mostly taken up by a large V-shaped double berth. On the starboard side, a bunch of planks were smashed in, and some of her ribs were damaged too. But most of her other timbers looked okay. I'd check it all out properly once I got the right tools up there.

Back in the main cabin, there were patches of rot in the underside of the decking, caused I guessed by rainwater leaking through the corrugated iron roof above. But an initial inspection of her cross beams gave me hope. I'd only know for sure when we got the rotten decking off her.

I climbed back out to the cockpit. Her rudder was badly damaged, whatever had struck the bow must have smashed her rudder too. That wasn't a big deal, we could replace the whole thing in one piece. The condition of her keel, main ribs, and stringers would be the deciding factor. The doctor was waiting below.

"Well, what do you think? Can you bring her back or not?"

He looked like a man awaiting a verdict in a courtroom.

"She's a big boat, Patrick. I'll need another man with me, a shipwright I mean. But if her keel is sound, and most of her ribs and stringers are okay, I feel sure we can bring her back, same as we did *Erin*."

"You'd find shipwrights over in Galway," Lorcan joined in, "I have a few contacts over there."

"You hire whoever you need, Conor. Just so long as you're the man supervising the work, I'll be happy." He glanced at his watch, "So, what would be your first move?"

"I'll be checking her keel later today. If it's sound, I'll move inside and go over her ribs and stringers. After that we'll have a better idea as to where we're headed. How long are you here for?"

"Two nights, then I'm back to Galway on the morning ferry."

"Okay, so why don't we meet up for breakfast the day you leave. I'll have a full report for you by then. After that it'll be up to you to decide what you want to do. As to costs, I'd only be able to guess, and it would be a wild guess at best."

"I know what it costs to rebuild a boat, Conor. But if you can do with *Anam Cara* what you did with *Erin*, the money will be the least of our worries."

✧   ✧   ✧

LORCAN HARDLY SPOKE on the way home, but as soon as we were seated at the kitchen table he began.

"I didn't want to say too much in front of Patrick," he was setting out cups, "but you seemed awful sure of yourself up there."

"Look," I said, "It's a bigger boat, but if her keel and ribs are sound, I feel sure we can fix her."

"So you said, but that deck's rotten, m'boy, through and through. And some of those cross beams would have to have rot in them as well."

"Lorcan, whatever it is, it can be fixed. Trust me. We'll do it one day at a time, one plank at a time."

"Conor, you need the job, I understand that, but every time you said *we* up there, I felt uneasy."

CHAPTER 8

Anam Cara

'Our character is built on the debris of our despair.'
Ralph Waldo Emerson

AFTER A HURRIED lunch, I retrieved my bicycle from the boatshed and cycled back up to Reagan's farm. A leather bag full of tools slung over my shoulder, the conversation with Patrick Finlayson playing over and over again in my mind. Could I save her? The boat was twice the size of *Erin*, and, if the truth were told, in worse shape. If she's too far gone, I'd have to tell him that before he leaves the island. I pushed the fear away. Giselle was counting on me.

I pushed the barn doors open, then hesitated on the threshold. *Anam Cara* stood quietly in the gloom, like a faded memory from a long-forgotten dream. The morning's optimism had been fueled by desperation, and Lorcan had made it clear that he had reservations.

"Could you not go back to your work in Australia?" He'd stared at me over the kitchen table. "Just for a year or two, I mean. Make some money over there to help your wife?"

"The company's gone, Lorcan. I was lucky to avoid bankruptcy. I'd be starting over from scratch. It would take a year or more for me to get back on my feet in Sydney. Giselle needs help now."

"Well, go up there and have another look." He stood up. "But leave your rose-tinted glasses in your pocket. You can't start a job you know you can't finish. Dr. Finlayson and his family are highly respected here on Inis Mór. You need to remember that."

I paused at the foot of the ladder, reluctant to view the chaos again. Then I changed my mind, got out the brace and bit, and began working on the keel. The wood was hard, but as I progressed, the pale-yellow shavings curling around the drill bit looked as fresh as the day the keel had been laid. I could smell the timber as it writhed it way out, the clean fresh scent of oak. All in all, I drilled eight holes, not a suggestion of rot anywhere. The keel was as true as the day it had been laid.

Emboldened, I climbed the ladder, my heart faltering again as I looked down into the cabin. Lorcan's words echoing in my mind, "take off the rose-tinted glasses." I pushed through to the for'ard cabin and began checking, the damage was obvious. Six or seven of the planks had been stove-in on impact, shards of splintered timber still standing stiff and erect. Next, I examined her damaged ribs. Only three were broken right through and would have to be replaced. Several of the others were cracked, but I felt sure that I would find a way to repair them. The broken planks would be a similar job to the work I'd done on *Erin's* hull. Probably not as difficult, as access would be easier. I went back to the shattered ribs. A few would have to come out and be replaced, but all in all, I told myself, the damage was not as bad as I'd feared.

I went through to the main cabin and began checking the underside of the decking. Slivers of light, slipping in between gaps in the planking, casting faint patterns across my hands as I reached up to test the cross beams. I knocked a couple of times with my knuckles, then moved further into the cabin and tried again. Tapping a little harder, not sure of what to expect. Maybe it's okay, I thought, maybe some caulking here and there. The sort of stuff you buy in tubes. That might be enough to fix some of the problems. I found a screwdriver in the toolbox and began prodding at the underside of the deck. So far, so good, I thought. Emboldened by success, I jabbed harder, but then, to my horror, the screwdriver, my hand, and half of my arm went clear through the decking, creating a hole as big as the mouth of a bucket, showering me with bits of rotting timber.

"Jesus Christ!" I said out loud.

"What was that?"

The voice rose from somewhere below and I clambered back up into the cockpit. The widow Reagan was standing by the ladder, a tray in her hands, and I wondered for a moment had I cursed.

"Oh, Mrs. Reagan, don't come up! I was just talking to myself."

"Ah, it's a sure sign of madness," she giggled, "but we all have a little of that in us, do we not?" She raised the tray, "There's tea and scones there for you now, Conor, it's the best I can do on short notice."

"No need to come up," I called out again, "I'm on the way down."

"I've never been up there in my life and never will. I'll leave it here on the bench for you. When you're finished talking to yourself, it'll be there waiting for you."

I watched her leave, then returned below, my heart still thumping. *First, you need to calm down*, I told myself. *One day at a time, one step at a time.* That's what the old man had said. It's not a life and death situation, I told myself, you're just rebuilding a boat. Breath in, breath out, calm down, remember what he said, "You can recover from almost anything, one day at a time, one step at a time."

✧ ✧ ✧

I worked on *Anam Cara* till three that afternoon, probing her timbers cautiously, terrified of repeating the morning's disaster. My heart faltering each time I encountered rot, lifting again when I struck solid timber. But after testing in dozens of places I began to hope that I had struck the worst part of the coach roof earlier on that day.

It was not good, it was a long way from good, but, with a bit of luck, and the right help, there was still a chance that I could take the job on in good conscience. Cycling back to the Reardon's place, I decided not to stay another night. I knew Mary would protest, but I didn't want to spend the evening fielding questions from Lorcan.

"But you will have dinner," she said, "I have it made special for you."

"I will, Mary, but I need to be back at my place tonight. I have things to prepare for Patrick."

"What sort of things?" Lorcan had been quiet until then.

"I need to make a few sketches. You know, pinpoint some of the major problems and how I intend fixing them."

"So, you still think you can handle the job?"

"Too early to say," I told him, "I tested the keel this morning and it's as solid as a rock. I drilled in a dozen places, not a trace of rot anywhere."

"And above?"

"Well, there's the damage to the decking and coach roof. But I don't think it's as bad as it looks. Then you have the planks that were stove in for'ard, but they won't be a problem once we've fixed her ribs."

"So, you reckon you're up for it?"

"I think so," I was regretting staying on. "Like you said, if we can get a good shipwright over from Galway there's no reason why we can't rebuild her."

"Mmm," he'd been avoiding my eye, but now he looked up, peering at me over the top of his reading glasses. "And you checked the coach roof thoroughly?"

"I wouldn't say thoroughly," I told him, "But I'll have a full report for Patrick before he leaves on the ferry."

"Well, aren't you a great support." Mary was staring at her husband, hands on hips. "Sure, you sounded like a born-again boatbuilder just a few days ago! Conor's doing the best he knows how up there. Wait for the report. Then you may have some idea as to what you're talking about."

"That was before I went up there, Mary. You'd need to take a look yourself. That boat stinks of rot and I don't want Conor making a fool of himself."

✧ ✧ ✧

IT WAS WELL after dark when I returned to Tír Na Nóg. The cottage stood still in the moonlight, faint shadows playing across her whitewashed walls. Traces of smoke rising from her chimney. I eased in through the door sideways, carrying a wicker basket of groceries Mary had given me, and what remained of my coffee supplies from *Erin*.

✧ ✧ ✧

I STAYED UP till three the next morning, drinking coffee, calling friends and associates in Australia. Putting out feelers as to the chances of finding a reasonably well-paid job in the cutthroat, dog-eat-dog, advertising world of Sydney.

CHAPTER 9

Rot

WHEN I ARRIVED at Reagan's barn the following day, the big doors were open, and walking through I found Lorcan by the bench, with Gráinne.

"Good morning to you, young sir," she looked uncomfortable, "Lorcan's here before you, as you can see." She turned. "I'll get you some tea." She left quickly, leaving Lorcan and myself staring at each other.

"You didn't tell me the truth, Conor."

"You've been up there?"

"I have. It was clear to me last night that you were hiding something." He was shaking his head. "It's a lost cause, m'boy. You're way out of your depth. Michael Greely was right. She's only fit for burning."

"You don't know that," I told him, "I still think there's a chance I can fix her."

"Conor, we live here. You can't be kidding the doctor on that you can fix this boat. She's beyond repair, and I think you know that. Look, I talked to Mary last night; we have some savings. Not a lot, but we can help. With your wife I mean. But I can't be involved in this, and I'll be telling Patrick the same."

"Lorcan, give me till this evening. I'm going to go over every square inch of her today and I'll tell you the truth. I swear I will. I didn't lie to you last night, but I did withhold stuff, and I'm sorry about that. Don't talk to Patrick yet, please. At least give me until tonight."

"You'll need to convince me, Conor. Dr. Finlayson's family are old friends. I'm compelled to be truthful with him." He stood up. "We love you, boy, and we feel for you. But you're a desperate man, and desperate men are not to be trusted."

He left without another word, and I sat there in despair. No matter what I told him tonight, it wouldn't change his mind, and it would not change the condition of *Anam Cara*.

Ten minutes later the widow was back, carrying a tray covered over with a blue and white checkered tea towel.

"Where's Lorcan," her eyebrows raised, "is he gone home?"

"Yes."

"So, things are bad up above?"

"What did he tell you?"

"It's what he didn't tell me that has me worried. He was banging around up there like a madman. I hope to God, you can set her right. She was in my care all these years, but there was nothing I could have done after Donnacha died."

"The doctor understands that." I told her, "I'll fix her yet if I can."

"God willing, so you will. I'll leave you be now to get on with it. Do the best you can, Conor, that's all any of us can do."

I took my time over breakfast. Fresh Irish soda bread, butter, marmalade, and a mug of hot tea, and for half an hour, I allowed myself to dream of happier days. Taking *Erin* offshore for trials. The voyage to Brittany, and the days I spent sailing with Tristan.

But soon breakfast was done, and it was time to face reality. Take off the rose-tinted glasses, I told myself. You have obligations here. You can't go back to being a con man.

I climbed the ladder slowly, feeling as if I was climbing towards the guillotine, then I sat in the companionway, my feet hanging down into the cabin, staring at the wreckage below. It was lighter down there now, and I realized that Lorcan had pulled away more of the rotting decking. A hole big enough for a man to crawl through, was now shedding light down among the debris. I stepped down into the main cabin. It was a disaster zone. The floor covered in bits of rotten timber, clouds of dust mites still hanging in the air, an undeniable smell of rot.

Well, that's about it, I thought, she's too far gone. So, what options are left? Maybe sell *Erin*? I could now, I'd been on the island long enough. Or maybe sell the cottage and keep *Erin*. Australia was a long shot; Giselle needed money now. How long would it take to sell the boat? I wouldn't know where to start. The cottage would be easier, an agent could handle that. I sat there, staring down into the doomed hull, despair settling around me like a heavy blanket. How could it have come to this?

"Is that you down there, boy?"

I spun around. The old man was standing above in the cockpit, the long black overcoat and cane.

"Jesus!" I burst out, "I thought you'd left the island."

"You were the one that left," he smiled.

"I was over in Brittany," I told him.

"Welcome home," he nodded, "and your wife and child, you didn't bring them back with you?"

"No, her mother's not well, she's looking after her."

"And your son?"

"My boy's fine."

"We need to talk about your family one day."

"What do you mean?"

He ignored the question and climbed down into the cabin, looking around, "So, what do we have here then; another boat to fix?"

"No," I said, "she's too far gone."

"Then why were you drilling into her keel?"

"That was yesterday," I told him, "Before I found all the rot."

"Is it sound?"

"The keel?"

"Yes, her keel,"

"I believe so."

"And her ribs and stringers?"

"The same, mostly. There's some damage to her hull for'ard, and a few of her ribs are broken, but the rest of the boat's too far gone."

"What makes you say that?"

"Take a look," I told him, "The coach roof's falling apart,"

"Let me see,"

I moved aside as he picked up the awl and began prodding the timbers.

"You're wasting your time," I told him.

He ignored me, reached up, and tore a lump of wood off the coach roof.

"That all needs to be stripped out."

"I know that!" I said, "But what's the point? If the entire

coach roof is rotten, why bother?"

"The coach roof, as you call it, has little or nothing to do with the boat. It's an addition, see here," he banged his cane on one of the heavier beams at the side of the cabin. "That's the original structure right there. She was built as a turf boat; the cabin was added years later when they converted her to a cruising vessel." He pointed a finger. "Pass me that hammer." I did. "Now, stand back." And suddenly he was swinging the hammer, once, twice, three times, breaking through beams and decking alike.

"Whoa! Stop!" I tried to grab his arm, but he jerked away. "Stop, for Christ's sake, stop!" He ignored me, bits of rotten wood flying about in all directions. He was moving quickly, as a man half his age, and he didn't pause until he'd cleared a section, from one side of the boat to the other. When he finally stopped, he took up the awl and began probing the beams he'd exposed.

"There you are," he jabbed the tip of the awl into one of the heavier timbers, "Oak, one of the best boatbuilding timbers there is, resistant to rot, gribble, and teredo worm." He turned. "Look, that's the original *Anam Cara* right there, solid oak. The rest," he waved a hand around contemptuously. "Added by carpenters, not shipwrights. A fancy looking cabin built out of cheap pine or the like. A timber acceptable perhaps for the inside of a house, but useless on a seagoing vessel."

"So, you know her original name," he did not reply. "Do you think she can be saved?" I could hear the desperation in my voice.

"Of course she can be saved. All she needs is a little care." He paused. "Now, you need to pull out every piece of pine you can lay your hand too."

"But you think I can rebuild her?"

"Not by yourself, no. She's too big. Get yourself over to the mainland. There are still good men over there building wooden boats."

"Will you be here too?"

"I may, occasionally, it's a two-man job if it's to be done right."

✧ ✧ ✧

I STAYED BELOW after he left, confused by this sudden change in fortunes. He claimed the boat was sound and I went over the heavy beams he'd exposed, testing, and retesting with the awl, probing, and prodding. He was right, the original timber was solid and virtually impenetrable.

I set too then with the hammer. Breaking away the coach roof in clumps, pulling out the rotting cross beams, tossing everything over the side. Stripping out every piece of pine, hardly pausing until I was knee deep in rubble. It was hard work, but I felt tremendous exhilaration. *Anam Cara's* original structure was now exposed. Dirty, dusty, and tarnished, but as strong and true as the day she was first launched. I almost wept with relief.

"Are you there, Conor?" the widow was back, "There's tea there for you… God Almighty what have you done?"

I jumped up on the bunk. She was standing by the barn door, tray in hand, staring up.

"I'll be right down, Gráinne." I told her. "Leave it on the bench if you would."

But she was there waiting for me when I arrived.

"What have you done, Conor! What will Patrick think?"

"Don't worry," I told her, "It was all rotten. But tell me, is there someone with a truck to get rid of the rubbish?"

"No need, the shed's coming down. He's arranged to have the whole place demolished. His wife's heart is set on a garden, you know, flowers and the like. Just toss any rubbish over the side and push it over into the corner out of your way. It will be carted away with the rest."

✧ ✧ ✧

AFTER LUNCH, I started back in. Breaking out rotten beams, removing what was left of the cabin, tossing the debris over the side, then sweeping out the cobwebs, chicken feathers, broken eggshells, and straw. By four o'clock, her hull was clear, so I went below and began wheelbarrowing loads of debris over to a corner of the shed. By five thirty, it was done.

The old man reappeared shortly after, staring up at *Anam Cara* before I realized he was there.

"Is it clear above?"

He didn't wait for an answer, and I followed him up the ladder.

"There you are now," he was smiling, "that's the original boat right there," he stepped down into the open hull, and I watched as he began testing, poking his little knife into the oak. Making a mark occasionally in chalk, muttering to himself at times. Eventually, he paused and turned.

"Everything here," he indicated, "every crossbeam, every plank, and every rib, are sound, bar for those few at the bow that we know of."

"The chalk marks?" I asked.

"There's some darkening around a few of the fastenings. It's to be expected. They'll be replaced with the rest."

"You're sure I can rebuild her?"

"With help, yes. Some of the side decking is worn, and will need to be replaced, but the cross beams underneath are sound. Once that's done, you'll check all her fastenings then strip her back to bare timber. The final work will be the new cabin, above and below, but any decent shipwright will know what to do there."

He left shortly after. I tidied up, put out the lights, then cycled down to Cill Rónáin to see the Reardon's. Boson greeted me as always, pushing past Mary, his rear end thrashing about.

"Come in, Conor," a slight frown telling me Mary was expecting the worst as we settled into chairs around the kitchen table.

"So," was all Lorcan said as they waited for me to speak.

"I think it's best you come up there," I said, "it's hard to explain."

"No need, Conor. *Anam Cara's* a right off. I think we both know that."

"She's not," I told him, "Come up tomorrow morning and see for yourself."

"You're still hoping I'll tell Patrick you can fix her?"

"No. I want Patrick to see her as she is now. He can make his own decisions then."

"Fair enough, but he's no fool, Conor."

"I know that, and I have her ready for inspection."

"You seem awful sure of yourself,"

"The old man turned up today," I told them, "The old man who helped me with *Erin*."

"Jesus, Conor, who is this man? Does he have any idea at all as to what he's talking about?"

"Stop that, Lorcan!" Mary looked shocked, "That same man rebuilt *Erin* with Conor. He's a retired boatbuilder, for God's sake. So, if his opinion differs to yours, I know who I'd be listening to!"

"Lorcan, I know you think I'm fooling myself, but you'll understand better when you see for yourself. Let Patrick know, and I'll meet you up there first thing in the morning."

"Fair enough, but I'll be giving him my honest opinion, Conor, and I expect you to do the same. You did a great job with *Erin*, we all know that, but that boat is a major undertaking, and you know you don't have the skills to do it right. You must tell Patrick the truth, the whole truth, Conor. We owe him that much at least."

CHAPTER 10

Gráinne

THE FIRST GLIMMERS of light, filtering in through my cottage windows, found me at the kitchen table. Sketching a new rudder and detailing other stages of the work. Listing types and dimensions of the various timber we would need, along with rough estimates of the times involved.

When I arrived at the Reagan's cottage, Gráinne was sweeping off her porch steps, her long black dress swishing low over the cobblestones, moving like a dancer in her soft leather shoes, sunlight glinting off her glasses.

"Maidin mhaith," I called out.

"Maidin mhaith, Conor," she paused, "Will we being seeing the doctor today do you think?"

"He'll be here any moment," I told her, "Don't worry Gráinne, I believe we have it sorted."

"Please God you do. The boat was there for so long I just took it for granted it was done with."

"The doctor's grateful to you," I told her, "And the boat's going to be fine, so don't worry."

"Do you need the tea now?"

"No, better wait until he arrives, he won't be long, he's catching the morning ferry."

I crossed to the barn, and as I swung the doors open, the

sun's early rays enveloped *Anam Cara* in a golden light, and I stood there for a moment admiring her lines. Then I went inside, spread my drawings on the bench and arranged my plans. I was still adding final touches to the diagrams when Patrick arrived, followed closely by Lorcan. They both appeared hesitant, and I wondered as to their conversation on the way up the hill.

"Good morning, Conor," Patrick attempted a smile, "I believe things are worse than we thought?"

"No," I told him. "They're actually a lot better. Go up and have a look for yourself."

"Is the coach roof gone?" Lorcan was staring up, mouth wide open.

"What?" The doctor stepped back a pace or two to get a better look. "Jesus, Conor, what have you done?"

"The coach roof was rotten, Patrick, through and through" I pointed to the corner, "That's it over there. Go up there now if you would, it's the only way you'll understand."

"Mother of God, Conor!" Lorcan was staring at me wide eyed. "You hadn't the right!"

Patrick was climbing the ladder, so I followed him up, wanting to explain. But by the time I caught up with him he was standing in the cockpit, staring at the gaping hole where the cabin had been.

"So, she was a turf boat originally," he was nodding, "And the cabin an addition."

"Yes," I told him, "And it was built from cheap pine, and that was the only part of her that was rotten. Everything else you see here is oak. No major structural damage except for half a dozen planks and a few ribs. There's not a trace of rot in her anywhere now, Patrick."

He was nodding, taking it all in.

"You're a bold man, Conor. I'll give you that." He turned and looked me straight in the eye, "But can you bring her back? The way she was, I mean."

"Yes, I can," I told him, "Once I get a good shipwright over here, we'll build the coach roof back the same as it was, only better."

"Well, labor shouldn't be a problem."

"Doctor," the widow reappeared around the barn door. "There's tea there for you now, when you're ready,"

"God bless you, Gráinne," he called back, "You're a fine woman, so you are."

When we climbed back down, I went to show him my sketches, but he held up a hand.

"No need for the sales pitch, Conor," he smiled, "I have every faith in you." He was searching through his wallet. "Look, I'll be gone from Ireland for the next three months or more. I'll put you in contact with Gwen, she's my personal assistant. She'll be responsible for getting you anything you need. Money, materials, whatever it is. Anything you need, call her."

"She'll be overseeing the work?"

"No, you're my man, Gwen's only there to assist." He handed me a business card, "Those are her details. You tell her what you need and leave the rest to her."

"There's one more thing," I paused, hoping to God I wasn't going to blow the whole thing, "Lorcan asked me to be completely honest with you. I'm not a boatbuilder, Patrick. *Erin* was my first effort, and I had a lot of help from an old seaman I met here."

"Titles mean nothing to me, Conor. I saw the quality of the work you put into *Erin*. Just so long as you're controlling the job, that's all I need." He smiled, "So, what's your next move?"

"Well, I have to get *Erin* up into Lorcan's shed for the winter. After that's done, we'll get *Anam Cara* in alongside her."

"Leave that to me," Lorcan was wanting to make up lost ground, "I'll call in to see Fergal on the way down. With a bit of luck, we'll have both in the shed within a day or two."

"Good," the doctor held out a hand, "Anything you need, Conor. Anything at all. If you must talk to me, give Gwen a call, but only if you must, I'm a busy man."

"Come on now, Patrick," Lorcan was squinting at his watch, "You'll not have time for the tea. Hennesy's skippering the early ferry, and he's the devil for punctuality."

✧   ✧   ✧

I SPENT THE rest of the day preparing for the move. Gráinne couldn't do enough, in and out with tea and food, delighted that the problem was solved, by four o'clock I was done.

CHAPTER 11

The Old Fort

WALKING HOME THAT evening, I noticed the signpost to Dún Aengus and on impulse turned off the track, climbed over a low stone wall and struck off to the West. The fields were a dozen different shades of green, dotted here and there with winter wildflowers. Rabbits pausing to stare, eyes wide, ears raised. Age-old walls crowned with moss. Tiny pools of rainwater, resembling miniature lakes, calm in the hollows of the stone. Miniature forests of lichen growing in their depths. Their varied hues and colors, differing in every way from one patch of flora to the next. Individual, natural wonders, like little hamlets along a boreen, inhabited by different tribes or species. Each determined that their own little kingdom would shine brighter than the rest. All of the same origin, yet as individual and enchanting as unrelated Fairey tales. All affirming the power that gave them be. All singing one song and one song alone; *This am I, this am I, pause now awhile with me.* And moving through that field, my Soul, infused by the beauty of it all, rose from the mundane to the transcendent, and in that freshened place, I saw the world anew.

The light was fading as I approached Dún Aengus. The sun almost touching the horizon, its golden glow caressing the ancient limestone walls, and as I passed through the entrance,

I spotted the old man. He was standing at the edge of the cliff, staring out across the ocean, his cane held in both hands behind his back.

"It's a fine evening," he turned as I approached, "although there is weather on the way."

"Brigid thought you'd left the island."

"Ah, Brigid," he chuckled.

"So, you do know her?" He didn't answer. "Do you actually live on the island?" Again, no response. And after a long pause I said, "Can we work together on *Anam Cara*?"

"I'll be there from time to time," he smiled, "but as I told you, my best days are behind me."

"Maybe just to advise?" I asked.

"Another man is coming, Con Rua, a good man," he gestured, "let us sit by the fire."

I followed him across to a small campfire that was burning on the ground and watched as he added logs.

"Draw closer, boy," he gestured, and I sat down on a large rock close to the rising flames. The light was fading fast, the first stars beginning to show themselves high in the firmament above. The old man tapping out the ashes from his pipe on a nearby rock. Then taking out his leather pouch he began fingering through the tobacco, as if selecting particular leaves. After filling the bowl, he tamped the tobacco down level with the rim of the bowl, took a sliver of wood from a log, lit it from the fire, touched the flame to the top of the bowl, and drew the pipe to life. Smoke billowing around his shoulders like familiar old ghosts gathering for a story. Once he was happy with the pipe, he raised his eyes to meet mine.

"And Brittany?"

"It was difficult." I told him, "I have no French, so I couldn't hold a job. Giselle works in a café six days a week, then spends most nights looking after her mother."

"And your son?"

"We spent some time together. I took him out sailing a few times."

"And you talked?"

"Yes, we talked," I paused, not sure I wanted to discuss Tristan. "It was awkward. I mean, I love him, but I felt as if there was a barrier between us. It's hard to explain."

"He doesn't trust you. You're a voice on a telephone." He paused, holding my eye, "An absent husband and father."

It hit me in the guts, but I knew he was right.

"So, how do I get over that?" I asked.

"Time. Time and patience. You never had a father of your own. You don't know how to bring up a boy. We will talk more of that another day."

"Giselle's beginning to trust me."

"She's a Celt, they are strong women."

"I didn't realize how strong," I said.

"Some of the greatest of the Celtic warriors were women," he nodded, as if satisfied, "Boudica, Scáthach, Gráinne Ní Mháille. That rock you are sitting on is known to some as Gráinne's chair. Many a time she sat right there, holding forth with the Chieftains of Inis Mór."

"Gráinne Ní Mháille?"

"You don't know the name?"

"No, should I?"

"Come over here, boy."

He rose, and I followed him back to the edge of the cliff.

The last strands of light were falling across the ocean, faint slivers of sunlight barely visible on the horizon, seabirds drifting home to the rocky ledges for the night.

"These waters," he raised his cane and swept it in a wide arc, "and the entire West Coast of Ireland, were controlled by Gráinne Ní Mháille for many years. She was known to the English as Grace O'Malley, the pirate Queen of Ireland. Respected not only by them, but also by the French, and the Spanish. She was a fierce warrior and would attack any ship that dared enter her domain. The English lost warships and men to her, and their navy learned over the years that it was wiser to avoid the West Coast of Ireland.

"She terrorized ships from Derry in the North to Killarney in the South, taxing all those who fished or traded those waters. Once, on a voyage to Spain, just a few hours after giving birth to a baby below decks, her ship was attacked by Corsican pirates. Hearing the uproar above, she leapt out of her bed, strapped on a cutlass, took hold of two pistols, then burst out on deck screaming like a banshee. Shooting and slashing at the invaders so fiercely that they lost heart and within minutes were retreating. Half of them were slaughtered trying to escape, the rest driven overboard and left to drown, while Grace and her crew seized their vessel as a prize of war.

"But her friendship with the Spanish led to complaints that her ships were plundering British vessels, and a price was put on her head by the Crown. But in a daring move to forestall the gathering storm, Grace sailed into the Port of London with just a handful of men and presented herself at the Court of the English Queen Elizabeth. The move was so bold that Elizabeth agreed to meet with her. It is said that when they met at

Greenwich Palace, Grace refused to bow because, as she told Elizabeth, she herself was a Queen, and therefore not subject to the Crown. Their discussion was carried out in Latin, as O'Malley spoke no English and Elizabeth had no Irish."

"Quite a woman," I said.

"And your wife?"

"I'll be calling her tonight to tell her I have the job. She needs money. Her father's an old man and he's not well. It could go on for years."

"What could go on for years?"

"Giselle's looking after her mother. Her father's incapable of working. He forgets things, you know, repeating conversations, rambling, Alzheimer's I guess, it's a mess."

"So, you're still thinking of yourself, boy."

"She's, my wife!" I felt a surge of anger, "And I want us back together. Is that wrong?"

"It's neither right nor wrong," he smiled, "just somewhat selfish. Your wife's another Grace, boy. Fighting to protect her family. And you, Con Rua, are the only warrior she has left to rely on." His dark green eyes held mine as he spoke. "She needs a partner, a friend. Someone she can depend on, in her time of need."

"That came to me on the boat," I said.

"Say more about that."

"It was during the gale. I hadn't slept for days. I had a dream; well, it was more like a hallucination."

"Go on," he was leaning forward, his pipe in his hand, the smoke from the fire curling in circles like a living thing between us.

"I saw things in the sea. Weird things, horses' heads, a

man's hand holding out a silver branch…"

"And?"

"I realized that the trip had been mostly about me. What I wanted. What I needed."

He laughed suddenly, and it startled me, "You think that's funny?"

"It is both sad and amusing." He was shaking his head, "But you're right, boy, you're still thinking of yourself." He lent towards me, his voice soft and low. "You lay with your wife, Con Rua. You and she are one again. Is that not what you wanted?" I didn't answer, "Legend has it that, in times of great distress, if a sailor has a good heart, the sea God, Manannán mac Lir, will rise from the depths of the ocean in a chariot pulled by two great horses and allow the poor man silver branch thinking. The ability to see both sides. You were blessed, boy. You were given a vision. You saw both sides, hers, and yours."

"I'm not sure I want to see both sides," I told him, "I just want my wife and son back."

"A man's first impulse must be to serve the feminine."

"You're saying that men should serve women?"

"Yes, but not the way that you're perceiving it," he smiled, "I'm saying that once a man has embraced that part of himself that is feminine, then he can no longer dishonour his wife, his mother, nor any other woman. Nor can he dishonour the same in any other man."

"How so?" I asked.

"The Soul is feminine, Con Rua, and the call rises from the very depths of our Souls. Whispering soft and low in both sleeping and waking dreams. Once you've accepted the feminine aspect, only then can you engage the masculine. Power wedded to integrity; strength tempered by the gentle heart. Therein lies true masculinity. Therin resides the holy union, male and female aspects working together. Feminine intuition, sensibility, and compassion, combined with truth, direction, and penetration with trust from the masculine. Without the feminine aspect, the male is more machine than man, blundering through life without any real feelings or any true purpose in life."

"Like Cu Chullain."

"Yes, like Cu Chullain; before the death of his son opened his heart."

"So, I stay on Inis Mór, and Giselle and Tristan stay in Brittany?"

"For the moment, yes," he was studying my eyes. "You are grounded now, boy, of the earth, and you must shoulder the burdens of manhood. The woman you love has given herself to you once again in trust. The work you have ahead of you will become the foundation on which you will rebuild your family and your life."

"So, the job becomes my calling?"

"No," he stared across, "That job will be the *vehicle* for your calling. It is the work you will do that will enable you to follow your calling. Do you not see? Your calling is something apart. The call is your life's purpose, the work your Soul longs to do. The mission that came with you to earth. It represents the essence of who and what you are and arises from the very depths of your being."

"So, it's a religious thing?"

"No, not necessarily. The concept of calling arose long

before formalized religious beliefs. The call is grounded in that ultimate source, the Soul, the Life Force, call it what you will. Our calling is an integral part of who and what we are. It accompanies us to earth at birth as the poet Wordsworth said,

Our birth is but a sleep and a forgetting
The Soul that rises with us, our life's Star
Hath had elsewhere its setting
And cometh from afar
Not in entire forgetfulness
And not in utter nakedness
But trailing clouds of glory do we come
From God, who is our home.

"Those clouds of glory contain your gift and your life's purpose. Irish myths spoke of the call a thousand years before the birth of the Christ in a legend known as the Myth of Oisín. Others followed. The great Irish hero Cú Challain is a fine example of a man following his purpose in life."

"But the story of Cú Chulainn's just a myth, isn't it?"

"You can never say, *just a myth*. All the great myths began as stories, Conor. True stories. Stories of men and women like Cú Chulainn and Gráinne Ní Mháille. Stories of ordinary men and women, rising above fear to protect their families and their people. Myths are accounts of heroic deeds of self-sacrifice. Myths speak of triumph and tragedy, and of the heroism that lies latent in the heart of every human being. The great myths speak of loss and redemption and remind us that there is always hope and the possibility of ennoblement, no matter how bleak the situation may appear to be at times.

Those original stories, repeated over campfires for millennia, arose in every culture from the beginning of time. Letting us know that we are not alone, that we are all connected, and that it is possible to follow the paths of the heroes and heroines who have gone before us." He paused to relight his pipe, smoke swirling around his shoulders as he drew it back to life. "Those stories first became legends, then myths. And those myths contain the distilled wisdom of humanity and have the power to inform and enrich all of our lives."

"So, what's the Myth of Oisín about," I asked.

He stared at me for a long time, then looked up at the night sky.

"It is late," he stood, "The Myth of Oisín can wait another time."

Then he nodded and strode off into the darkness without another word.

CHAPTER 12

Slipping *Erin*

WE SLIPPED *ERIN* two days later; the forecast was for storms, so we began at dawn. Fergal and his men strengthening the old cradle. Reinforcing the timber uprights, checking all fastening, Lorcan hovering, watching every move.

We dragged her up out of the water just before midday, the tractor's wheels churning up pebbles on the beach as it strove to get a grip. The rain increasing as the day wore on, Lorcan calling out commands, Fergal ignoring him, confident in his craft.

Once she was up on the hard, the rest was easy, and by three pm she was safely back in the boatshed, moved over to one side to allow room for *Anam Cara*.

"Is there time enough to get the doctor's boat down?" Lorcan asked.

"No," Fergal was shaking his head, "I've enough of rain for one day. Weather allowing, we'll start in on the Doc's boat at seven in the morning, time now for a pint of porter."

✧ ✧ ✧

IT WAS CLOSE on midnight when I arrived home. We'd started off at the American Bar on the waterfront, but an hour later the front door flew open, and a wild-eyed head leaned in, accompanied by a blast of wind and rain.

"The craic's fierce up at Joe Watty's," it yelled, before disappearing back into the night like some disembodied messenger from the Otherworld. He might well have called out *fire* for everyone in the bar followed as one, rushing up the road through the pouring rain, some still clutching pints of Guinness.

As we arrived at Joe Watty's Pub the session was already going strong. A massive fire burning in the hearth. A tall, rangy looking man with a wild shock of black hair was sitting on a bench playing the uilleann pipes, a woman to his right a fiddle, the man next to her thumping away on a bowran. Tim at the end of the table, giving it stick on a tin whistle.

I stayed with them for a few hours, but there's only so much mineral water you can drink, and with the volume increasing, and the dancing growing wilder, I called it a day and slipped quietly out a side door. The pounding drumming of the bowran, the haunting wail of the uilleann pipes, and the rising strains of the fiddle, following along behind me through the wet and winding lanes.

✧ ✧ ✧

SEVEN AM CAME and went the following morning, and with the rain increasing, and the constant rumble of thunder, I figured they'd called it off for the day.

I kept myself busy, collecting tools, sweeping out the shed. Getting everything ready for the move. But just after nine, I heard the roar of a tractor and moments later Fergal appeared around the barn door, his men trailing along behind.

"Good morning, Conor."

"How's the head?" I asked.

"A man who never drinks is always well," he declared, his bloodshot eyes at odds with the statement, "Lorcan's not here?"

"No. What time did you finish up last night?"

"Around two, I think. He wasn't fit to stand. We had to see him home. Mary was not amused."

"The weather won't stop us?"

"No, we need to get it done. The center of the storm's a day or so away yet, but when they come in slow like this, they hit hard," he waved a hand, "Get to it now lads, we don't have all day. Check every bolt on that cradle, Michael. And Darragh, start in on those skids. Make sure they're on good and tight now, it's a way down to the boatshed."

Three hours later, we were ready. Steel skids bolted to the underside of the cradle, chains attached at the front, heavy cross beams adding stability to the frame. Fergal reversing the tractor into the barn. His men removing the wooden gates to the yard from their hinges. Gráinne fussing around as they worked.

✧ ✧ ✧

WE MOVED *ANAM Cara* out of the shed slow and steady. The men, swathed in oilskins, stamping their feet on the ground against the cold, breath hanging in the air. Fergal easing the boat down towards the quay, pausing occasionally while they removed rocks from the path. I had fears that she'd be too high to clear the entrance, but they were unfounded, and by four that afternoon she was safely ensconced in the shed alongside *Erin*, her cradle sitting firmly on solid ground.

CHAPTER 13

Repossessed

WHEN I ARRIVED at the hall Wednesday evening, the meeting had already begun, so I found a chair and joined the group. The same people were there plus two I had never seen before, with Fiona O'Shea chairing the meeting. The priest was present and as soon as the meeting began, he stood up.

"My name is Father Aiden, and I'm here to tell you all that this program works," he declared, "I had my last drink just a week ago, and I've already had a spiritual awaking! It was if I was possessed by the divil and now I'm a free man!"

"Sit down, Aiden," Fiona was having none of it. "And don't drink one day at a time or you'll be repossessed!"

Later, over coffee, I sat with the priest and suggested we go over the program.

"There's no need, Conor, I already have a good grasp of spiritual matters."

"It might help you understand the disease of alcoholism," I told him.

"Conor, I know you mean well, but after I left you in the boatshed that day, I read Romans, Corinthians, and Galatians, and as I read, I felt the power of God coming into me. And I know now that I was put on this earth to bring lost souls back to the Lord."

"Aiden, you're only off the drink a few days; okay? Nobody wants to listen to your raving."

"You're a hard man, Conor, so you are!"

"I'm trying to help you, Aiden. Drop into the shed anytime." I told him, "And keep coming back," I told him, "You'll get right if you try."

CHAPTER 14

The Myth of Oisín

I was pulled from sleep the following day by heavy rain battering my bedroom windows. I sat up reluctantly and peered out. Sullen, purple black thunder clouds were moving ponderously across a storm-tossed ocean. Melding ominously with the darkening waters and obscuring any trace of a horizon. While lashing rain, deafening rolls of thunder, accompanied by vivid flashes of lightning, confirmed that the center of the storm was upon us.

I dressed and went below. The embers in the hearth were barely alive. I spread kindling wood on top, fanned the fire back to life, then loaded it up with logs, hoping that would be enough to keep the chill from the cottage until I returned. Then I prepared bacon and eggs and drank coffee as I waited for a break in the weather.

As soon as the rain eased a little, I pulled on my leather jacket and oilskins and made a dash for Cill Rónáin. Peddling furiously along the laneways. The fields sodden, the cattle, huddling together against stone walls, wide eyed with fear.

I peddled as if my life depended on it. Sliding around corners, wet as a shag. Skidding through muddy patches, tearing down slopes, reveling in the mad dash for cover. As I rounded the final rise, I spotted smoke rising from the shed's chimney and knew that the old man was there. Stepping through the door, I found him sitting by the fire, staring into the rising flames.

"Maiden maith" he looked up and smiled.

"Good morning," I said, "it's dark in here." As I threw the light switch, there was a sudden flash and a popping sound, and the lights failed. I went across to the fuse box, the wires were smoking.

"The circuit's blown," I told him, "And I'm no good with electrical stuff."

"Don't worry, boy, there's not much you could have done here today."

I organized candles close to the fireplace, then put the kettle on. By the time I returned with the tea, he was sitting in his chair, eyes half closed.

"Your tea," I passed him a mug.

He nodded a thank you, then we sat there together for a while staring into the flames.

"I've been thinking about what you said, about having a calling. Most of us ignore it, right?" He didn't answer, "For various reasons, I suppose, with me it was money. Pretty dumb, I guess."

"There's no need to make it right or wrong," he shook his head, "Many well-meaning people are led astray by circumstance. Life has a habit of getting in the way of our dreams."

"You mentioned the Myth of Oisín," I said. "If it's so important, why haven't I heard of it?"

"A fair question," he nodded, "perhaps it was forgotten, or more likely, held from us. The idea of every human being having their own purpose in life does not sit well with those who would lead us in other directions. You see, following your heart sets you free, Con Rua. Free to become the person you were born to be."

"And Oisín did that?"

"The myth's not so much about how Oisín lived his own life, but how he performed a duty that has enabled millions across the ages to find their destinies," he took a long draw on the pipe, then settled back in his chair, "Oisín was an Irish warrior, stuck down on a battlefield in the pride of his youth," his eyes narrowed, as if remembering. "Seven days later, long after the fighting was over, soldiers of the Tuatha Dé Dannan roamed the battlefield, retrieving the bodies of their fallen comrades. But when they came upon Oisín, they were confounded, for although clearly dead, his body had not given way to decay. They examined him every which way, but to no avail. So, they carried the body to the funeral pyre, said the prayers for the dead, and cast him up among all the others.

"But the moment Oisín's body touched the flames, he started back to life and leapt out of the fire. The soldiers were confounded, and they took him to the Druids, and there he recounted what had happened to him in the Otherworld. He told them that when the life force left his body, he found himself standing in the field that surrounds the Hill of Tara, along with hundreds of others.

"There were all types of people there, people of all ages. On one side of the field, lush green grass fell away to a calm, clear river, parents and children playing in the water, talking and laughing. While on the other side of the field, there was a great black cavern belching clouds of smoke and flames. And as he watched, bedraggled people came staggering forth, their clothes charred, their faces set and grim."

"Heaven and hell," I said.

"Perhaps," he nodded, "Then Oisín caught sight of the Goddess Ceridwen, and her daughter Taliesin, sitting on a throne, high on the Hill of Tara. And by her side the Cauldron of Wisdom, the great bronze cauldron that contains all the wisdom of the world. And as he watched, she rose from her throne and struck a single blow on the cauldron with a golden hammer and the crowd turned as one and fell silent. Then she reached deep into the cauldron and brought out jars filled with lots, each bearing a number. And moving closer to the gathered crowd, she scattered the lots among them. Tossing them high into the air at random, repeating her actions three times. Now the lot that fell closest to you was yours, and that gave you a place in the proceedings.

"Next, three great, snow-white storks appeared in the sky, each carrying in their claw's baskets laden with feathers. Flying in from the east, circling the meadow three times before emptying their baskets down over the assembled multitudes before disappearing back from whence they came." He paused to draw on his pipe, "Now on each of the feathers, painted in the finest gold filigree, were the names of various careers, lifestyles, or professions. One feather bore the word, *Carpenter*, on another, *Cleopatra, Queen of the Nile*, on another, *Teacher*, and on yet another *Artist*. Every possible trade, or occupation was there, and there were thousands more lives to choose from than there were people present on the meadow. Lives of soldiers and sailors, schoolteachers and doctors, missionaries, merchants, and kings and queens. Every type of life lay before them, and it was for them to choose the one that appealed to them the most."

The old man paused, and took several puffs on the pipe before continuing, "Now, once those souls decided upon a particular life, they were joined in that instant by a *Daimon*, what some might call a *Guardian Angel*, or *Soul's Guide*. And in that moment *Daimon* became their lifelong companion and the host and carrier of their calling.

"Now the people from heaven chose their new lives quickly, laughing and joking with each other, but the people from the dark cavern did not. Those people picked up one feather after another, carefully considering each possible life, terrified that they may once again make a choice that might open them to grief. And once they were all done, they went in the order of their given lots before the Goddess Ceridwen, who then wove the threads of purpose and passion into the lives they had chosen. Once done, their choice was ratified and irrevocably sealed.

"Then they were told to face the sun, and as they did, the heavens lit up with a great white light. Blinding them in an instant and erasing from their memories everything that had gone before. They forgot their previous life, their death, and their rebirth. They forgot about the life they had chosen, and they forgot about their personal *Daimon*, that aspect of the divine that was to accompany them to Earth. And in that instant of forgetting, each of them was driven high into the sky and forward to their new lives, like shooting stars across the firmament.

"Oisín himself, however, did not go with them, and by what means he returned to earth, he could not say. But that morning, waking suddenly, he found himself lying on a burning pyre."

"So, it's suggesting that our lives are predestined," I said, "that we don't have any choice in the matter."

"No, quite the opposite," the old man smiled, "for the Gods give each of us free will. They insisted on that. And though the choice you make is irrevocable, what you do with that life is entirely up to you. It is up to us whether we live out our potential in a meaningful or a destructive way."

"So, if…"

"Whisht now," he held up a hand, "understand this; the *Daimon* joins your soul because it has a purpose in life, a mission to fulfill. Something that will benefit the world and its people, but it needs your cooperation to achieve its aims." He was staring at me intently, *The Daimon, chooses the family into which you are to be born, knowing what will happen to you in that family.* Now, some families spoil their children, but no discipline means no real love, for discipline is an essential ingredient of love. In other families the child may be abandoned, abused, or worse. But know this, in surviving whatever happens to you in your family, you are unconsciously developing the skills and talents you will need to fulfill your calling, the meaning and purpose of your adult life…"

"Are you suggesting that people who have been abused should be grateful for that?"

"No! Do you not see? Myth offers a reason and a meaning to suffering and the possibility of ennoblement! The myth, if properly understood, offers redemption, Conor! We've discussed this before; do you not you remember?

Blame not your kin, hold not to grief
No matter what was borne
Your Purpose lies within your reach
And with your Soul was formed
Those childhood days you chose yourself
Your Soul intent on learning
But unless you rise to meet this call
You will go forever yearning."

"But if we forget about the *Daimon,* and our purpose in life, what's the point?" I asked.

"We forget, yes," there was a glint behind his dark green eyes, "but the *Daimon* does not forget. And your *Daimon* will call to you at different times throughout your life. Whispering to you that you are wasting your days working at things you have no real interest in. Pulling at your heart, telling you there is more to life than this. Calling you back to purpose, to meaning. The call may come while staring up in wonder at a starry night. Or when you are at your lowest ebb and your life is falling apart. You may read a book, or watch a moving picture, and be stirred by the call. It may come as the still, small voice, whispering, '*Is this all there is, Is there no real purpose to my life?*' You see, boy, the call comes from the very depths of our souls. Calling on each of us to wake up and remember our mission. Calling on us to remember the *pre-natal agreement*." He paused for a long moment, holding my eyes with his, "The events of childhood, no matter how painful, mold, shape, and prepare us for the potential genius of our adult lives."

I was thinking back to my father's death. The shock and grief that followed. My mother's refusal to mention his name. The pain of leaving Ireland and everything I knew. The bleak, empty years in Australia, feeling abandoned by the world. Never knowing who I was. The unhappy household I lived in after my mother remarried. Hiding in my bedroom reading books. Making up stories, living in a fantasy world. The nagging suspicion that there was something wrong with me. That I was not enough. The grandiosity I developed to protect myself. Taking up boxing, to prove that I wasn't afraid. The endless struggle to be heard, to count. My twisted relationship with my wife. The way I'd ignored my son for much of his life. And my own never-ending needs and wants. Holes in the soul I tried to fill with flashy cars, fancy clothes, alcohol, and drugs.

The old man stood, tapped his pipe out on the hearth, and headed for the door.

"It's lashing down out there," I said.

"Remember this, boy," he turned to face me, "if you remember nothing else, remember this. You were molded, shaped, and prepared for the genius of your adult life by the circumstances and events of your childhood; no matter how painful those days might have been."

I spoke without thinking, "There'd be many who'd disagree with you."

"There would indeed," he smiled, "And there'd be many who'd live to regret that. Try not to be one of them."

✧ ✧ ✧

I SAT THERE after he left, mulling over what had been said. My first reaction was to dismiss the idea, but then I thought of my storytelling. That was where it began. I must have read a thousand books in that bedroom. The family spent most evenings in the living room, but I stayed away, unsure of my place in the household. My other refuge was the library. I spent hours there, devouring stories that engrossed me. Later, I began writing. Pages where I was looked up to and respected. The only class I ever topped was English literature. One teacher scrawled on the bottom of a report card, "he has a gift." That was where it all began. That was where I was molded and shaped for the meaning and purpose of my life. That was where the seeds of the seanachaí were sown.

CHAPTER 15

Brigid O'Neil

THE BEDROOM WAS cold when I woke. Pure, crisp, white frost framing the edges of my windowpane. A brisk sea breeze kicking up whitecaps as far out as I could see. Strands of sunlight filtering through low hanging clouds offering hopes of a better day.

The fridge was all but empty, so I made coffee, pulled on a sweater, and propped myself out at the end of the crumbling stone wall at the back of the cottage, my breath visible in the frigid air.

The view from our apartment in Sydney had been the envy of our friends, but this was different. The Atlantic Ocean thundering against this rock-bound shore. Waves surging in, endlessly and forever, seabirds floating sentinel above. It's ever-changing moods adding a savage granduer to an ocean at once both staggeringly beautiful and unconscionably cruel.

I drank another coffee, made out a shopping list, pulled on my bomber jacket, then jumped on my bike and rode to the store. The front door was wide open as I arrived and walking in, I caught the sound of raised voices from the back room.

"Are you there Brigid?" I called out.

Nothing, but the voices continued, louder now. Not wanting to eavesdrop, I went back to the door, closed it, then jerked it open again, the bell on the frame jangling somewhere in the back of the store. A moment later the curtain was thrust aside, and Brigid appeared.

"Good day to you, Con Rua, and what brings you to my doorstep this fine day?"

"Good morning, Brigid."

"There's stuff for you there, over from Galway on the ferry."

"Do you know what it is?"

"Hardware. Boxes of nails and stuff. It should have been left on the quay. It was brought up here by mistake and it weighs a ton."

"I'll get someone here to bring it all down."

"Tessie will bring it down for ye'."

"Tessie?"

"Tessie, one of my ponies, I have two of them. I rent out pony and traps in the summer. You can keep her at your place for the winter if she's any use to you. There's not enough grass here for the two of them anyways."

"I might do that," I told her, "Thank you."

"So, what is it you'll be needing today?"

I handed her the list and there was a long silence as she studied it.

"So, you're wanting bread, tea, sugar, milk, eggs, rashers and a tin of baked beans," she looked up. "Sure that's not enough to keep body and soul together for more than a day or two at most."

"I need some meat, a couple of steaks and a chicken if you have them."

"We do of course, frozen that is. You'd get your fresh fish

down below from the fishermen. They're off out again today I believe."

I watched as she bent headfirst into a deep freeze, pulling out the various items, bundling them up in newspaper, then counting out the eggs.

"You mentioned that you knew a boatbuilder over in Galway."

"Yes, Quinn Cullen. Born and bred here on Inis Mór. He took a job over there years ago, and the next thing we knew he was married. Trouble was he was already engaged to a young woman here. He broke the poor girl's heart, so he did. We never saw hide nor hair of him again. Too ashamed to show his face no doubt."

"Conor, it's yourself!" the priest appeared from behind the curtain, a bible in one hand, "I thought that was your voice."

"Morning, Aiden, how are things?"

"Never better," he smiled, "All the more so for seeing you."

"Are you going to the meeting tonight?"

"No Conor. No need. Sure, I haven't touched a drop since the day we last met. Myself and Brigid here were just about to begin a Bible Study. Would you care to join us?"

"Pay him no heed," Brigid had her hands on her hips, "He's here every second day waving that book at me. He won't take no for an answer." She turned to the priest, "I have my own relationship with God, and what that is, is none of your business! Do you not hear me? Jaysus, you were a better man with a drink in ye."

"Now Brigid, don't be taking the good Lord's name in vain. You're not long for this world, and you need to be making your peace with your maker while you still can."

"Get out of my shop!" she grabbed a broom and took a swipe at the priest, "Go on, get out, get out or I give you a skelp!"

He made the sign of the cross in the air, as if warding off evil spirits, then ducked and made a dash for the door, Brigid after him with the broom, "And don't come back here!" she shouted after him.

"Are you okay?" I asked.

"I'm fine, he's either mad drunk or out to save the world. He's a good-looking lad, I'll give him that, but he's no craic at all sober."

✧ ✧ ✧

AFTER DROPPING OFF the supplies at home, I unhooked Tessie from the trap, left her in the garden, then headed down to the Reardon's cottage. Boson let out a few barks as I approached, then recognized me and offered apologies by way of his mad rhumba-bum dance and bulging eyed smiles.

"Come in, Conor, no need to knock." Mary was swathed in an oversized pale blue dressing gown with a woolen collar and cuffs, reading glasses in one hand. "Have you eaten?"

"No, but I've had coffee."

"Coffee's hardly enough," Lorcan appeared alongside her in the identical dressing gown, "I'll put on more eggs. We're just about to sit down for breakfast ourselves."

I sat with Mary, Lorcan fussing about, frying bacon, cracking eggs.

"I was up at the store just now. Brigid knows a guy over in Galway, a boatbuilder. She thinks you might know how to contact him."

"And his name?"

"Quinn Cullen."

"Oh, no," Lorcan turned from the stove, "Not Quinn, you'd steer well clear of Quinn. He's a fierce man for the drink altogether. The last time I saw him was in Eyre Square in Galway. Just out of rehab and begging for money on the street. That was three years ago, God alone knows where he'd be now."

"Brigid wouldn't have known that," Mary came in, "all she knows is Inis Mór. Although Madge was over there a few times, having her teeth done, I believe."

"There must be other boatbuilders over there," I said.

"There are of course," Lorcan passed a rack of toast to Mary, "Galway was a major shipbuilding area years ago. There you are now, Conor." He handed me a plate of food, "Get into that, we'll sort out your boatbuilders later."

✧ ✧ ✧

As soon as breakfast was over, he took me into his den, a small bedroom that looked more like a museum than an office. The Irish Tri Color held pride of place, surrounded by photographs of the Post Office under siege by British troops, a poster bearing the Declaration of Independence, underneath that pictures of Michael Collins.

He scribbled some notes, then I followed him back to the kitchen.

"There's three shipyards for you there now," Lorcan handed me a mug of coffee, then slid a sheet of paper across the table, "The man I just spoke to has no idea at all as to whether they can help you or not, but it's a start. They're all boatbuilders, if they can't help, they would know others that might. When are you going over there?"

"Tomorrow morning," I told him, "I have a meeting with Patrick's secretary in Galway. I need to get things moving."

CHAPTER 16

The Black Fitz

I ARRIVED ON the quayside at eight the following day. It was a cold, clear morning, brittle sunlight glinting over an untroubled ocean, seabirds wheeling overhead. Tim sitting on a rusting bollard clothed in a military greatcoat, a scarf and a woolen beanie, clouds of smoke rising all around.

"Good morning, Conor," he held up a hand, "will you join me in a puff?"

"Morning, Tim, but no thanks, I don't smoke."

"Neither do I," he smiled, his eyes disappearing into an impish grin. "I gave her my word that I'd never touch another cigarette, so I vape now, something she knows nothing of."

"Your wife?"

"Yes, she's a lovely woman, nobody likes her."

"You don't smoke at home?"

"God no, she'd have a fit. She's fierce about diet and such. She weighs twenty-five stone naked as Venus but has no shame at all lecturing the likes of myself. And me only eight and a half stone dripping wet."

"I don't think I've met her." I said.

"No, she's something of a recluse. Up at the mass every morning, rain, hail, or shine. Praying for old red socks and the Holy Roman Empire. Then off back home again to her little office, controlling the world on the internet. She has a heart of gold, or so I'm told, and not one bit of it for me."

"Sorry to hear it's not working out."

"Not working out," he was shaking his head, "Well, that's one way of putting it. Jaysus, she has my heart broke with her tongue."

I wasn't sure what to say.

"Have you considered a divorce?"

"Divorce!" he stood up abruptly, "Jaysus, Conor, that's a terrible thing to say! Sure, I'd be lost without her."

He tucked the vape in his top pocket and stomped off up the road. And, as I stared after him, the ferry let out a blast on its foghorn and people began filing on board.

✧ ✧ ✧

THE BUS WAS waiting on the quay at Rossaveal, and by midday I was at the front desk of the Skeffington Arms Hotel in Eyre Square.

"Just the one night, sir?"

The receptionist was tall and slim, her red hair, blue eyes and freckles telling the world at large she was an Irish woman.

"I'm not sure," I told her, "I'll know better by tomorrow morning. Could you arrange a cab for me for two pm?"

"Where to, sir? They'll want to know."

"Again, I'm not sure, I have to make a few calls."

After settling into my room, I went down to the restaurant, ordered a late breakfast, then dialed the numbers Lorcan had given me.

"Sullivan and Sons,"

"Hi, I'm looking for Dan Sullivan."

"Dan's away for a week or so. I'm his son, Tyrone. You're a friend of his?"

"No, my name's Conor O'Rourke, I was given your number by a friend. I'm rebuilding an old sailing boat over on Inis Mór and I'm looking for a couple of shipwrights to help me."

"You've called the wrong number so. We haven't built a wood boat here these past twenty years. None of the big yards do, it's all fiberglass now."

"Do you know anyone who still works with wood?"

"Well, there's a few around. You could try Finbar Fitzgerald. I believe he still builds a wood boat or two each year. He lives a few miles out of town on the road to Rossaveal. But be warned, he's a difficult man."

"Difficult in what way?"

"Ah, you'd be better off seeing for yourself. He's a good man, just a bit on the strange side."

I made a few more calls, but it was the same with all the other boatyards, everything was fiberglass. As I sat there mulling over my options, a middle-aged man in a tweed overcoat and cloth cap, approached.

"You called for a taxi, sir?"

"I did, but you're early."

"Better so than late," he nodded, "May I join you?"

"Sure, there's coffee there if you'd like a cup."

He sat down across from me and held out a hand.

"Gavin Hennesy, at your service,"

"Conor O'Rourke," we shook hands, "Nice to meet you."

He pointed a finger, "And the toast?"

"Help yourself, I'm done."

"Ah, you're a good man," He was buttering the toast liberally. "Some of the tourists are awfully stuck up you know, and it's a shame to waste good food."

"I'm not a tourist," I told him, "I'm from Inis Mór. I have a house over there."

"You have a house on Inis Mór?" he looked amazed. "Well, you'd be the only Yank in the world who could claim that."

"I'm Australian," I told him, "But I was born here in Galway."

"Well, sir, with respect, you'll need to decide which one you are now, for your own sake that is. And just because you spent time in Australia doesn't make you a kangaroo."

"You're from here," we were both laughing, "from Galway?"

"Born and bred," he nodded, "never left the place. My older brother Brian went off to America at eighteen and was never heard from again. Broke his mother's heart, so he did." He shook his head. "No. I'm happy where I am. Galway is the finest city in the world."

"How can you be sure of that if you've never been anywhere else?"

"Well, sure aren't you a good example yourself? You've been all around the world and now you're back here in Galway having breakfast with the likes of myself. There's tourists come here every year, Yanks, Germans, Australians, Canadians, you name it. And just about every one of them tells me that Ireland's the most beautiful country in the world." He smiled a crooked smile. "They can't all be wrong, sir." He finished off the last of the toast, then downed his coffee in one gulp. "So, where are we headed?"

"Do you know of a boatbuilder by the name of Finbar Fitzgerald? I believe he lives on the road out to Rossaveal."

"He does indeed. The Black Fitz. I know him well. And you're wanting him to build a boat for you, is that it?"

"No, I'm rebuilding an old wooden boat on Inis Mór, and I'm looking for a boatbuilder to give me a hand."

"So, you're a boatbuilder yourself?"

"No, not really. I was left a boat by my grandmother. Myself and an old seaman rebuilt her over there last year. That's the only experience I have, but this boat's twice the size."

"How big is she?"

"She's forty-four feet."

"Jaysus, that's a fair lump of a boat," he was leaning towards me now, "and her name?"

"*Aman Cara,*"

"*Anam Cara*! Sure, that was old Doc Finlayson's old hooker. She was wrecked over there years ago."

"Not wrecked," I told him, "They got her up out of the water before she could sink. She's been stored in a shed there since. You know her?"

"I do of course. Sure, everyone in Galway knows the story. It's what did the old Doc in, or so they say. He died just a year or two after. The son took over the business then, he's something of a go getter. Opened clinics all over Ireland, then went into property, hotels and the like." He was nodding, "So, he's the one paying to have her fixed?"

"Yes,"

"Well, Fitz would be the boy for the job. If he's not too busy with his poetry that is,"

"Poetry?"

"Yes, he's a Fili, a poet. He has the gift."

"How old is he?"

"Oh, he'd be around fifty I'd say. Maybe a few years either way. But don't worry about that, sure he's a bull of a man. I'm told he can get under a full-grown horse and lift him up off his four hoofs. But he's a strange one, sir, cut from a queer cloth."

"You know where he lives?"

"I do of course. He has a few acres out on the road to Rossaveal just short of Spiddal," he glanced at his watch, "I can have you there within the hour."

✧ ✧ ✧

IT WAS AFTER three when the taxi turned off the road, wound its way along a narrow dirt track, and came to a halt outside a large wooden shed. The building was surrounded by racks of timber, rusting machinery, and a few upturned wooden dinghies. The high pitch wailing sound greeting us as we stepped from the cab warning us that work was in progress.

"Now don't argue with him. Just state your case, tell him what you want, and leave it at that. He'll tell you straight if he's interested or not. But don't argue with him, he has a short fuse."

The first thing I took note of as we arrived at the entrance to the shed was a boat propped up in a cradle. She had similar lines to *Anam Cara*, an all-black hull, the single word, *Dierdre*, carved in intricate detail on the wooden plaque on her stern.

As we crossed the threshold, a young lad touched the shoulder of a short, thick set man who was pushing a long balk of timber through a circular saw. The man completed the task before turning. He was an extraordinary figure, almost as wide as he was tall. His body twisted to one side, the face partly concealed by an unruly mass of curly black hair, and a thick bushranger's beard flecked with sawdust. The first thing that struck me was his face. It appeared to be misshapen, with piercing blue eyes, one set higher in his head than the other. Both shining brightly, like warning signals to the unwary. As he approached, I realized by his gait that he was a hunchback, and my heart sank. He looked stone mad.

"Gavin," he nodded to the driver, then turned to face me, "And who do we have here?"

"Conor O'Rourke," I said, "I was talking to Tyrone Sullivan. He gave me your name. I'm from Inis Mór."

"Not with that accent you're not; more like Sydney Harbour I'd say."

"Close," I told him, "But I was born here in Galway. My father was an islander."

"You're an O'Rourke from Inis Mór?" his forehead furrowed, "So, you'd be related to Con Rua O'Rourke, the seanachaí?"

"I'm his son," I told him, "My mother moved to Australia after he died."

"God Almighty, sure I knew Con Rua, God rest his soul," he stared at me hard as we shook hands, "So, what brings you to my door?"

"I have a boat to rebuild on Inis Mór. I'm looking for a boatbuilder to help me."

"Well, you've come to the wrong place, so," he glanced at the cab driver, "And you should have known better than to bring him out here," he turned back, "I'm sorry, Conor, but

I'm no man's helper. I build boats, and only those I chose to build."

"Like this one?" I nodded towards the boat in the cradle.

"Yes, that's my own boat, and before you ask, no, she's not for sale. I've been promising to build that boat for an age. When things went quiet here last year, I thought it was now or never, and there she is. She'll be done within the month. That's her mast I'm just after cutting there now."

"She's a pretty boat," I said."

"She's a Galway hooker," he nodded, "a Bad Mór. You're a boatbuilder yourself?"

"No, I'm an amateur. I worked with an old seaman on my own boat, he did most of the work."

He gestured, "Would you like to look her over?"

I went up the ladder after him, the cab driver following on behind. Fitz had an easy rolling gate, his powerful shoulders swinging him up on deck like a trapeze artist.

"She's all but done," he gestured, "take a look below."

I climbed down into the cabin. It was a boatbuilder's dream. Beautifully carved wooden deck beams supporting planking that looked as if every piece had been handpicked. The bulkheads between each cabin perfectly set out. Gimballed brass oil lamps adding atmosphere and light. Niches for books behind the bunks. Intricately carved shelves in the galley.

"That's beautiful work," I told him.

"That's my son's work, Cillian, he's the artist in the family, I just build boats." His eyes narrowed, "So, what happened to the old man you were working with?" he asked.

"He's still over there, but I don't see him so often now."

"And his name? Do I know him?

"I'm not sure of his name," I said, "I know that sounds odd, but it was never mentioned."

"How old would you say he'd be?"

"Hard to say, but he'd be more than eighty I believe. Although he doesn't seem that old, if you know what I mean."

"No, I don't know what you mean. How tall is he?"

"Very tall, well over six foot."

"Tell me about this old man of yours, does he carry a stick?"

"Yes."

"And did he tell you stories?"

"Yes, quite a few."

He stared at me for a long moment, then turned to the cabbie.

"You can take yourself off home now, Gavin," he said, "I'll be driving Conor back to Galway."

"Jaysus, Fitz," the cabbie protested, "the first decent fare I've had in a month, and you're after cancelling the return trip on me!"

"Don't worry," I fished out my wallet and handed him a hundred euro note, "will that cover the return?"

"It will, and then some," he turned to leave, "Look after him now, Fitz, he's a decent man."

Fitz waited till the driver disappeared before turning back to me.

"This old man of yours, he wears a long black coat and an old seaman's cap; right?"

"Yes, you know him?"

"If it's the same man, I know him. Sure, didn't he teach me my trade here in this shed thirty years ago?"

CHAPTER 17

Quasimodo

AFTER RETURNING BELOW, Fitz sent his son off to the house, then told me his story. Born on the back seat of a car on a winter's night in Galway, snow drifting across an icy road. The father shouting back to his wife, "We're nearly there now darling, we're nearly there." Two blocks from the hospital, the car slid out of control, smashing headfirst into an oncoming semi-trailer at eighty miles an hour. By the time the ambulance arrived, the new mother was dead, the father unconscious, and the newborn left with a crushed skull and shocking injuries to his body.

When his father was released from hospital three days later, a priest and a surgeon were waiting. Together they walked to the children's ward where the deformed child lay unconscious in a glass incubator. They talked for over an hour. And when it was suggested that it might be better for all concerned to turn off the life support and allow the boy to die a natural death, it was said that the only one who had protested was the priest.

After seventeen months and countless operations, there was no more to be done, and the child was released back into his father's care.

As Fitz recounted the story he never once met my eye. He

smiled occasionally, always at the most tragic parts. A habit developed in childhood I suspected. For the next few years, they lived alone on their little acreage, seldom having friends over. And, as children do, he grew up accepting all things as normal, never considering himself odd or different. It was only when the time came to begin school that the problems began.

"You see, I was looking forward to the schooling. I'd see the other lads on and off the bus every day, laughing, having the craic and I couldn't wait to join them. The first day at school they stayed away from me, but by day three the older lads were calling me Quasi, you know, Quasimodo, The Hunchback of Notre Dame," he smiled again, "I belted one of them, after that it was home schooling."

"Your father taught you?"

"No, sure he had no schooling himself. No, they had a retired teacher come in three times a week, just a few hours each day. The school arranged it, they were glad to have me hid away I suppose," the smile again, "but she was a great woman altogether. She took her time, you know? Introduced me to reading first, then poetry. It was the poetry that held me. She had me reading Katharine Tynan, William Butler Yeats, Oscar Wilde, and James Joyce among others. By the time I was ten, I was writing poetry of my own."

"And you're still writing poems?"

"I am of course. It's a blessing and a curse."

"How so?"

"Well, it was the poetry that brought me to undone," his voice softened, "You see, they began publishing my work. First here, then over in England. Then an American agent took me up and had me published over there. I once never showed my face in a book. I didn't want to be frightening the children," the smile flickering on and off, "I had people writing to me from around the world, America, England, everywhere. Mostly women, but some men too. I'd read their letters if I ever got depressed. My father passed away when I was twenty-three. After that I lived here alone for years." He stood up and walked to the open doors, that odd swinging gait. Standing there still for a while, as if wondering whether to continue or not. When he finally returned, he smiled again.

"Well, one day I noticed a letter from Inis Mór on top of the pile, the postmark caught my eye. It was from a young woman in Killeany. She'd bought one of my books and said it had touched her heart. I wrote back," he shook his head, "I should have known better. Soon we were writing regular. I lived for those letters. If I didn't hear from her for a week, I'd be in bits, wondering if someone had told her. About how I look, I mean. She sent me photographs; I sent her poems. She asked for a photograph, I sent more poems. Then one day, just before Christmas that year, she wrote and told me she loved me. Well, I was gobsmacked! I laughed, I cried, I ran through the fields out there like a madman. The most beautiful creature I had ever laid eyes on had said that she loved me. But I was terrified too, and I didn't reply for weeks. She wrote again, three times." He shook his head, as if trying to shake off the memory. "Finally, I wrote back and told her the truth. I told her I was deformed. I told her they called me Quasimodo at school. I told her that I loved her too, but that it never could be." There was a long pause.

"And that was it?" I asked.

"No, she wrote back. She told me that no matter how I

looked, she loved my heart, and that was all that mattered. She said she had never felt whole in her life before she read my poems. She swore that if she couldn't marry me, she'd remain single till the day she died, and she begged me to go over there and meet her."

"And you did?"

"No, not at first; I didn't have the heart. But I read and reread those letters. More came every week. She said I'd broken her heart, she said she had nothing left to live for. Finally, I went across there on the ferry."

"So, you did meet."

"Yes," he shook his head, "well, no. You see when the ferry arrived, I hung back. I let all the passengers off ahead of me. I'd have gone back home if I could have, but it was the last ferry. I saw her waiting below on the quayside. Long red hair and a white dress. Finally, I got up the courage. I went to the head of the gangway and waved down to her," his voice was failing, and I knew that he was back there on that gangplank, "and that was that."

"How do you mean, what happened?"

"She froze, that's what stays with me. She froze for a moment, then she turned and ran."

"Da," Cillian appeared at the side door of the shed, "Ma wants to know if you want tea?"

"Not just now, son, maybe later," we watched as he ran back up to the house, "He's a good lad, just after finishing school. He did well in the finals but refuses to go further. All he wants to do is to work with wood."

"Is there any way I can persuade you to come to Inis Mór?"

"No. It wouldn't be fair on the wife, she's happy here." He

paused, unsure of himself, "He just disappeared you know, the old man. Neither a word nor a nod. He just disappeared."

"When did you meet him?"

He stared across at me, as if wondering whether to answer or not.

"That same day. I got off the ferry and walked. At the end of the quay, she'd turned right, so I turned left. I have no idea how I ended up at Dún Aengus. It was like a nightmare that was refusing to end. But the next I knew I was up there on the cliffs, looking down at the rocks below."

"You tried to kill yourself."

"Yes. I had no idea until I was there on the edge. There were voices. Voices telling me it was the best thing to do, encouraging me to step over."

"What stopped you?" I asked.

"A hand on my shoulder. The old man."

"Da," his boy was standing by the open doors again, "dinner's nearly ready. Ma wants to know is the man is eating with us or not."

"No, he's not. Tell you ma I'll be a while," he turned, "Go home, Conor, I'm not your man. Jump in the car, I'll get you back to Galway."

CHAPTER 18

Gwen

I was at breakfast the following morning when Gwen arrived, striding across the restaurant, hand outstretched.

"Conor," she smiled, "sorry to be late. I've had a mad morning. Patrick's having a few problems in New York, but the teleconference is not till midday, so we have time."

She was around thirty-five, a smart looking black woman of medium height. Brilliant white teeth standing in stark contrast to her skin, boy-short hair, black blazer and slacks, a blouse all the colors of the rainbow, and a rolling drawl that told me she was from somewhere south of the Mason Dixon line.

"You've eaten?" I asked as she took a chair across from me.

"No, I'm not a breakfast kind'a gal, but I wouldn't say no to coffee."

We chatted for a while. She was Texan, born and bred, her parents, immigrants from a war-torn area of Nigeria.

"Patrick told me you were born here?" She was smiling, sizing me up.

"Yes, we moved to Australia when I was eight, first time back."

"Well," she reached for a leather folder, "down to business. So far, I've had no luck. There are a few shipwrights available, but none of them want to work on Inis Mór, or at least not for that length of time. Patrick told me it could take four months, possibly more, but…" she was scrolling through notes, "I have two carpenters willing to take the job on, though neither have any boatbuilding experience."

"No," I told her, "They had a carpenter over there a few years ago to work on my boat and it was a disaster. Carpenters work in straight lines, you know, doors, windows, floors. Boats are all compound curves, arches, bent planking."

"Got it, but that's all I've come up with so far. How about you, any luck?"

"No, I met the perfect guy yesterday. He's building boats out on the road to Rossaveal, but he's not interested in going to Inis Mór."

"That would be Fitz, yes? Finbar Fitzgerald?"

"You know him?"

"Oh yes, we know Fitz. We went out there last year, Patrick and me. He's a hard man to forget."

"And?"

"Well, how should I put it? He was blunt. Apparently, he'd told Patrick not to go out there when he'd called earlier, but Patrick doesn't understand the word *no* when he wants something. Patrick's father was one of the doctors who worked on Finbar after the accident. You do know what happened to him?"

"Yes, he told me."

"Well, things got a little tense. Finbar's very direct. He told Patrick that he was grateful to his father, but that he owed Patrick nothing. We were there for over an hour, but he made it clear that he wouldn't consider working on Inis Mór."

"Did he say why?"

"No, but he was adamant, so we had to leave it at that."

The waiter appeared with fresh coffee. As he was pouring, my mobile rang. I checked the number, private.

"Conor O'Rourke,"

"Can you make it out here for dinner tonight?"

"Finbar?"

"Yes,"

"Tonight?"

"Yes, my wife wants to meet you."

"You've reconsidered?"

"I didn't say that I said my wife wants to meet you."

"Okay, I'll get Gavin to drive me out, what time?"

"Around five or six," he hung up.

"That was him?" She was wide eyed.

"Yes, he invited me out to dinner tonight, said his wife wants to meet me."

"Did he say why?"

"No."

"It has to be about the boat."

"No idea. He said yesterday that he'd never set foot on Inis Mór again."

"Again?" Her eyebrows furrowed, "He told us he'd never been to Inis Mór."

✧ ✧ ✧

I SPENT THE rest of the day exploring Galway. The city has a rich and colorful history. Many of the galleons from the Armada were wrecked on the West Coast when the defeated

Spanish fleet, caught in a heavy gale, were driven onto the rocky shores around Galway. Some of the survivors made it to shore only to be killed by the Irish, others were spared and settled around Galway to become what is known as the Black Irish. Remnants of the black curly hair and dark skin, still popping up from the gene pool generations later.

Finbar's call had me baffled. He'd been clear that he would never set foot on Inis Mór again, and I understood why. I couldn't begin to guess why his wife wanted to meet me.

Gavin appeared at four thirty and put me through the usual inquisition as we drove out to Spiddal.

"So, you're invited back out there; that doesn't happen often with the Black Fitz. Did you meet the wife?"

"No, but apparently she wants to talk to me."

"Well, and don't repeat this, sir, if you got a shock with Fitz, be very careful when you meet his wife."

"She's deformed too?"

"I'll say no more," he shook his head, "I'd hate to be on the wrong side of Fitz."

As we turned off the main road, Finbar's boy spotted us and retreated into the boat shed; Fitz appearing moments later, a length of timber in one hand, an axe in the other.

"You're early," he declared, "I'll finish up here now and be with you in a moment."

I paid Gavin off then followed Fitz up to a low stone cottage surrounded by bushes and flowers. The front door was painted bright red with a large brass door knock which Fitz thumped on several times.

"Just to warn her we're here," he nodded, "and behave yourself,"

I was still considering that when the door opened, and I was taken aback. A tall, slim, dark-haired woman stood there, her skin a pale, translucent white, her face serene. One hand on the doorframe, the other resting lightly on a hip. She was wearing a long, dark green dress that touched her feet before rising to a point just below her neckline. I was struck dumb, for she was without doubt, the most beautiful creature I had ever laid eyes on.

There was no pretense in her dark eyes, just a hand rising gracefully to greet me, and for an insane moment, I almost bowed and kissed it. Finally, I got myself together and we shook hands.

"I am Dierdre," she smiled, "And you are welcome in our home."

I followed her along a short hallway to a living area, Fitz close behind. The interior of the cottage was homely. The stern, limestone walls softened by bookshelves. A fireplace set deep in stone surrounds; a fire glowing in the grate. Several finely carved wooden artworks on stands, elegant, but not intrusive.

"Your son's work?" I asked.

"Yes," Fitz nodded.

"You taught him?"

"No, it comes natural to him. He draws too. We made up the plans for *Dierdre* as we went along."

"Dinner's ready," Dierdre's voice came floating out from the kitchen.

The table was set. A white linen tablecloth, bright cutlery, a carafe of water, three glasses, napkins in silver holders, a candle burning in the center.

"Take a chair," Fitz grunted.

Dierdre arrived carrying plates, and after saying grace she looked across at me,

"My husband tells me that you know the old man on Inis Mór."

"Yes, we worked together on my boat over there."

"How did you meet?"

I hesitated. I'd never talked to anyone about that day, not even Giselle. I'd told her about the old man, but I'd avoided the worst parts of what had happened on the clifftop.

"I met him at Dun Aengus…" she cut me off.

"No, from the beginning I mean. Start from the beginning. What brought you there, how it began."

I thought back, my life in Sydney all seemed so distant now.

"It's a long story."

"So, begin," she nodded.

I did. I told them how my life had fallen apart in Australia, drinking, coke, bankruptcy. Dierdre interrupting occasionally to ask a question.

"And you've never taken another drink?" or, "Do you still love your wife?" or, "Why did you call your son, Tristan, do you not know the story of Tristan?"

I told them everything. I wasn't sure why. When it came to the part about the old man saving me from the cliff edge, she interrupted again.

"Did he sing to you after?"

"Yes."

"What did he sing?"

"He sang in Irish."

"But what did he sing?" she asked again.

"I don't know," I told her, "I have no Irish. There were a few names I recognized, Tristan, my son; Giselle, my wife; my father's name, Con Rua O'Rourke…"

"No," she cut in, "No, he would not have sung of your father. He was singing to you, Conor. To bring you back to Inis Mór."

"But why?"

"You have brought something to us," her voice was soft and low, and I felt a chill brush alongside my spine, "something we do not yet understand. But it will come together on Inis Mór, as will our lives with yours."

"I don't follow," I said.

"What do you mean, acushla?" Finbar's eyes narrowed.

She turned to face him.

"We will go to Inis Mór."

"But why?" there was fear there, but no denial.

"Finbar, your poetry is grand, but not yet great, though I know you have greatness in you," she reached across the table and placed an open hand on his heart, "There is something missing, cushlamachree. You left part of your soul on that island, and I need it back here in my heart with me."

He stared at her, then back at me, and in that brief moment, I caught a glimpse of the terrified child cowering behind those fierce, shining eyes.

CHAPTER 19

Colette

AT THREE AM the following morning, I was pulled from sleep by my mobile shrilling in the dark. I checked the number.

"Giselle?" I could hear her breathing. "Giselle?"

"My mother passed, Conor."

"Oh, God, when?"

"Just now. I'm here with her."

"I'll come over tomorrow."

"No, there's nothing you can do here."

"I can be with you," I told her, "Does your father know?"

"No, not yet. His sister's here. They're very close. I'll tell her in the morning,"

✧ ✧ ✧

WE BURIED COLETTE three days later in the village graveyard. Mist shrouded mountains, heavy, snow laden clouds. Mourners in black overcoats and scarves. The men holding hats, the women touching handkerchiefs to their eyes. The same church bells that had welcomed her birth, tolling slowly for her passing.

The reception was held at the farmhouse, friends, and relations murmuring condolences. Giselle moving among the mourners, her father wandering around, confused as to what was happening.

"You can't stay here now, Giselle." I told her that night, "You can't look after your father properly, and Tristan's frightened of him."

"Dad's harmless, Conor, he's just confused," she was in tears, "Martine's moving back home as soon as she sells her place in Paris. She wants to look after him. They were brought up here together. He's just lost Mum, I can't leave him just yet. Don't ask me to, please."

"Then let me take Tristan. That will make things easier for everyone." There was a long silence, "Darling, there's a school on the island. He'll love it there."

I stayed for two weeks, doing odd jobs around the farm, walking in the hills with Tristan, exploring the ruins of an old castle nearby, visiting the local markets on Giselle's day off.

"I want to live with you, Dad, Mum can come later."

We were sitting in the living room, the open fireplace burning between two rooms in the French way. Giselle talking with Martine in the kitchen.

"We're talking about it," I said, "but your mother can't leave just yet."

"But Auntie Martine wants to look after him, she's coming back here to live."

"I know, but she has to sell her house first, and that will take time. Be patient son, it won't be long now."

I woke in the early hours, aroused from sleep by the hooting of an owl. The remnants of the fire casting faint shadows across the stone walls. Giselle's hand on my chest, her eyes glittering in the half dark.

"Another few months," she'd whispered, "just so I know he'll be safe."

CHAPTER 20

Galway

ON MY RETURN to Galway, I checked back into the Skeffington Arms. Fitz's wife had invited me to a night of poetry and there were things to be finalized. Gwen had offered him a generous package, so the money side was sorted, but I had to establish lines of credit with suppliers so that we could order whatever we needed by phone.

When I arrived at Fitz's shed that evening, Dierdre was setting up a table for refreshments, Finbar tending to a fire in a large steel brazier, their son arranging lanterns in the rafters above. A large swiveling captain's chair stood in the center of the room. An Irish harp and stool close by.

"He's not shy?" I asked.

"No, not anymore. He was years ago. He had no friends of his own and he's not good with strangers. But his old schoolteacher brought people out here. You know, one or two at a time, to listen to his poetry. There'll be fifteen or so here tonight. He knows them all and he feels safe with them," she threw back her head and laughed, "But no, once the spirit takes him, he's off, you'll see."

✧ ✧ ✧

FINBAR AND DIERDRE disappeared early that evening, leaving myself and Cillian to welcome their guests. There was no charge for the evening, just an old, galvanized bucket by the entrance, the single word, 'Contributions' scrawled on the side.

By five thirty everyone was seated, lanterns casting a soft glow over the shed, people talking softly, the boat acting as a backdrop to proceedings. A small oil lamp dangling from a cord directly above the chair in the center of the circle.

Dierdre entered at six and sat by her harp. She was barefoot and wearing the same green dress as before.

"To welcome you to our home," she smiled, "a song written by Phil and June Colclough called: 'A Song for Ireland.'"

As she began, the place fell silent. Her voice carrying throughout the shed. Her dark hair falling in waves across her shoulders. Her eyes glittering in the shadowed light. Her body moving in unison with the rhythm…

"Walking all the day, near tall towers
Where falcons build their nests
Silver winged they fly
They know the call of freedom in their breasts
Saw Black Head against the sky
Where twisted rocks they run down to the sea
Living on your western shore
Saw summer sunsets, asked for more
I stood by your Atlantic sea
And sang a song for Ireland."

She sang all four verses, and as the song drew to a close, the applause began. People clapping, comments called out in Irish. Dierdre stood and bowed, before holding up a hand.

"Thank you, but tonight is for poetry, another evening we'll be giving over to song. Until then," she swept her arm around behind her, "My husband, Finbar Fitzgerald…"

Fitz entered the circle, moving with that peculiar, sloping gait. One shoulder higher than the other, his head tilted to one side and slightly upwards. His powerful arms swinging front and back, one hand almost brushing the ground as he approached the captain's chair.

There was a hush as he took his seat. He cut an extraordinary figure. Dark green corduroy trousers and black boots. A heavy, cream-colored Aran sweater. A seaman's cap tilted at an angle, the black hair and beard as unruly as ever.

Dierdre kissed his cheek, then took her place by the harp.

Fitz sat there for what seemed like an age before he spoke, "For all those present who cannot speak Irish; shame on you!" There was a ripple of laughter among the audience. "Because" he continued, "these nights are conducted in Irish. This first poem is a true story of a woman who walked into the sea one night after hearing news that her husband had been lost from a trawler during a gale. It is called: A Fisherman's Wife."

A hush fell as he began. His voice taking on a deeper timber. His face softening as the words took him. One hand moving in the air as if conducting the flow of something at once both beautiful and tragic,

> "Now you lie cold beneath these waves
> that I should rise no more."

Dierdre was next to me, translating his words, her shoulder touching mine, electric sparks coursing up my spine as she whispered in my ear,

> "The vows we made return in grief
> Though we swore evermore
> Not knowing how the race would run
> Or if some keeper kept the score
>
> My heart is lost without you
> With you now cold alone
> I will not tarry to see you gone
> Away from our bright home
>
> For in that empty, lifeless place
> I would be the walking dead,
> For fear of letting go, my love
> For fear of letting go
>
> No, I will join you now, macushla,
> And swim far from this shore
> And we will lay there in the deep
> Together evermore."

I was studying Fitz. The oil light above casting a forgiving glow over features transformed from grotesque to a strange, ethereal beauty. His hand moving gently with the words. His bright blue eyes peering upwards, as if seeking inspiration in the shadowed caverns of the roof. The chair turning slowly, around, and around. The audience hushed and was silent till the last words sounded.

That was the first of several poems, and though I hardly understood a word of Irish, I sat there entranced. The session drew to a close at seven thirty, so I thanked them both and slipped away. I was booked on the early ferry back home and needed an early night.

Gavin drove me back to Galway, chattering away, "So, I'm told he's off to Inis Mór to fix Dr. Finlayson's old hooker. You must have offered him the world of money."

"We're talking about it," I said.

"Well, you have the right man. Now, what sort of money would it take to sort a job like that?"

"Not sure, Gavin, we'll know better in a month or two."

"But you must have some idea, sir."

I didn't answer, my head was still back at the boatshed. That hadn't been Fitz sitting in that chair, or at least not the Fitz I knew. And I realized in that moment that this was the *Daimon* that the old man had spoken of, the genius expressing itself through Fitz and the gift of poetry.

CHAPTER 21

The Dark Knight

THE DAY AFTER I arrived back on the island, I set about rearranging the boatshed. Fitz's workshop was laid out in an orderly way, and I wanted mine the same. The old man arrived late in the afternoon as I was wrapping up for the day.

"Good evening."

I turned, he was standing by the door, the collar of his greatcoat raised against the wind.

"Hi, I'm just finishing up for the day,"

"It's fierce cold out there."

"Will I make us tea?" I asked.

"If you have the time."

As I put the kettle on he tended to the fire, sliding the poker beneath the grate, raking out old ashes.

"There you go," I handed him a mug.

"Without a vision, the people perish."

"What?"

"It's an old proverb, King Solomon, I believe. A vision is but another term for a calling. Leaders like Solomon are few and far between these days."

"I always associated the term, Calling, with the English tales of Boadicea and King Arthur."

"Neither Queen Boadicea nor Arthur were English, boy.

They were Celts, as was all of Britannia in those days." He gestured with his pipe, "Sit, and I will tell you a story. And listen well, for it's one that every young man should know. He was staring into the fire as if seeking inspiration in the flames.

"This is a story that goes back before the strangers ever came to Ireland. Back before the written word was known of. Before Ireland was united under Brian Boru, our first High King." He paused, wisps of smoke from his pipe rising in circles around his head. "Ireland was a hardy place in those days. Different kingdoms spread across the length and breadth of the land. Warriors guarding each border and God help those that strayed into someone else's lands bearing arms."

Boson had woken up when the old man began talking and was now sitting on his rump staring up at him.

"One of those kings was Finn McCullough, known to be one of Ireland's fiercest warriors. It was said there wasn't a man could stand against him in battle. He'd inherited disputed lands from his father, but after many years of struggle, he finally brought peace to the kingdom. And in the years that followed, his lands prospered, his people were happy, and his queen bore him three children, two girls and a boy. The eldest was a son named Fianna, after that legendary band of warriors who protected Ireland's borders. And before the lad was old enough to court a woman, he was known to have inherited his father's skills with a sword." The old man paused and looked across at me. "He trained in warfare with the Soldiers of the Guard and sat with them around campfires each night. Listening to the stories of the battles they had fought and the victories they had won. And other stories, stories that many said were but old wife's tales. Stories of a strange Dark Knight, who lived in the forest just outside the eastern borders of the kingdom and was rumoured to possess great powers. And when they spoke of this knight, they spoke in whispers, and young Fianna began to dream of meeting this dark person and defeating him in battle.

Well, by the age of eighteen, Fianna felt himself ready to serve, but his father saw no reason to risk his only son's life in the skirmishes that still occurred around the borders of the kingdom, and he refused him.

"But father," Fianna protested, "I will be king one day, our people must learn to respect me for who I am."

But the old king knew that his son, inflamed by the passions of youth, would make him a hindrance in any army, for he was in the red stage of manhood, with all a young man's failings.

"You will do as you are bid," he told his son. "When you are ready to serve, will you be called."

Fianna was dismayed by this, for although he had the respect of his father's court, he knew they respected him only because he was his father's son. But then one day, a friend of his father arrived at court. A warrior of the Green Knights of Kerry, riding a war horse and bearing shield and lance. Well, Fianna was struck at once by the man's demeanour. Proud yet humble, strong yet serene; and that night after dinner, he sought out the visitor in his chambers.

"Dear Knight," he began. "I overheard your conversations with my father over dinner. You are a man of war, and yet you carry with you a sense of peace."

The old man's face was obscured at times by the haze of his pipe, but I could tell by his voice that he was going into one of his dreaming states.

"Well, at first the knight spoke but little, answering the young man's questions yet always seeming to avoid the issues. But the young man persisted and finally, late into the night, the soldier relented.

"You ask questions for which the answers are few. If I have seemed to evade you then it is for good reason. The path you seek is a dangerous one, a path not travelled by many."

"Sir Knight," the Prince persisted, "You have fought in many battles and have seen many things. I beg of you, guide me, for my purpose in life is a mystery to me." The knight stayed silent for a long time before answering, "Fianna," he told him, "you seek honour on the field of battle, yet have no idea as to who your enemy might be. You are a young man, in the fire of youth, and there are things that can be only revealed by time."

Hearing this, the young prince grew even more impatient,

"Then what are these things?" He demanded. "My father grows old, sir, we have already talked of succession. To take the crown now, I could but live in his shadow. The people need to respect me for my own courage, not my father's. Dear sir, I must have my day!"

The knight fell silent again, and the prince sat quietly, praying that his plea had been heard. Finally, after much thought the knight spoke again:

"You remind me of myself as a young man," he said. "It is a deeper wisdom you seek, though you cannot know that. It is not to be found in words, nor in the council of men." The knight hesitated, and when he spoke again, he said, "I can point the direction, but the path you must walk yourself." He looked up at the young prince. "You have heard of the Dark Knight?"

"I have heard rumours of a Dark Knight," said Fianna, "But whoever I ask denies the story, saying it is nought but rumour."

"And what does that tell you?"

"That they fear this man, which I do not. For I dream of meeting him on the field one day and defeating him in battle."

"Why so?" asked the Green Knight, "Why would you wish to do battle with a man you know nothing of?"

"He lurks on the boundaries of our lands, that is reason enough. And his death will prove that I am worthy to be king."

"Listen to your mind in matters of war, young prince, but strive also to understand your heart. For that is the only true direction you will ever have."

"But what does that mean?" The prince shook his head, "Understand my heart?"

"There are two parts to every heart, sire, the masculine and the feminine. The way of the masculine you already possess, but devoid of the feminine, that way will bring naught but grief."

"And how does one discover this feminine you speak of?"

"You must be willing to let go of your fixed beliefs and open your heart to others at times," the old warrior told him. "Both life and death, come from the shadows, and you must be willing to meet both, for both will come. I will give a poem, one that was given to me, the day I first set out on the quest:

It will come when you're ready

And when you are not

It will take different forms
You may believe them or not
The Lover, the Trickster
The Crone, and the Shrew

That is all I can give
The test is for you
Ride forth now young sir
With your bright sword and lance
But do not covet the throne
Until you have learnt how to dance.

The old man settled back in his chair and took a few puffs on his pipe before continuing.

"The young man rose before dawn the next day and took himself to the stables. There he saddled his father's warhorse, Fastus, a destrier stallion of fifteen hands. Snow white on its head and shoulders, jet black on the hindquarters. He prepared the horse for battle, chain mail around its head, its shoulders covered in steel studded leather, scaled metal armour buckled around its great chest. Then he assembled his own armour. A breastplate and helmet of steel, and a red and white shield emblazoned with the crest *Honour et Gloria*. Then crept into his parent's chamber whilst they slept and stole his father's sword, and as the day dawned, he rode from the castle gates. His horse trotting and prancing, the early morning sunlight glinting off his shield and lance.

The prince rode without pause, stopping only to eat and rest, and by the end of the third day he reached the forest that marked the southern extent of his father's lands. The forest was dense and dark, and it was said that no man had ever entered there and returned to tell the tale. Fianna rode this way and that, seeking a pathway in, until finally he came upon an old blind woman sitting on a log by a stream.

"Good evening," he called out, "Is there no path through this forest?"

The old woman looked up, her clouded and dull.

> *"Who comes to me now*
> *Is it friend or foe*
> *Speak kindly dear sir*
> *For your direction to know."*

The prince remembered the old knight's words and thought this may be help he needed.

"I am Prince of Ireland," he said, "In search of adventure."

The old woman laughed.

> *"Your demeanour is haughty, your courage runs high*
> *You seek your life's purpose, up there in the sky*
> *You dream of bold conquest, yet others must die*
> *To make you feel manly, to give you the lie*
> *You ride out in armour, a boy and a man*
> *A vision before you from which others have ran,*
> *The quest you are bound for, beware of the cost*
> *When you kill for no reason, whose life has been lost?*
> *The vision you seek, by the Dark Knight is held*
> *Your life may be forfeit, his dagger may geld*

> *You must move from the heavens, your cause lies not*
> *with the lance*
> *Do not face the Dark Knight, until you've learnt how*
> *to dance."*

"Speak clearly, old hag," the prince demanded, "You are on my father's lands and exist only at his favour."

But the old woman threw back her head and laughed,

> *"You are the young darling, the pride of your band*
> *Yet still you don't know, on whose legs you stand*
> *Your quest is for glory, your vision is vain*
> *But before you be king, you must know who you've slain*
> *When you ride out to kill, your honour you stain*
> *Seek not your own glory but take heed of Gawain."*

But the Prince had heard enough, and turning Fastus's head to the forest, he forced his way in through the darkening trees. At first, he could see but little, the trees were so dense. But after a few hours he came across a clearing and decided to spend the night there. He dismounted, tended to his horse, collected twigs for a bed, and ate the last of the food, before laying himself down to rest.

When he awoke the next morning, he found himself by a lake and after washing in its waters he saddled Fastus. But, as he was about to mount, a movement on the far side of the glade caught his eye, and a knight in armour, riding a black war horse moved from the cover of the trees. The prince knew at once that this was the Dark Knight of whom he had heard so much. The Dark Knight rode towards him slowly, his visor lowered, his black shield relieved only by a single, scarlet heart set in the very center.

"You trespass far from your father's lands," the dark stranger called out before dismounting.

"I am a prince of Ireland," he called back, "I ride where I will."

The two men studied each other, both well versed in the rules of combat.

"Your choice of weapon?" The Dark Knight called out.

"The sword," replied the prince.

"But I am master of the sword," the Knight replied, "for I know how to dance."

The prince, remembering the old crone's warning, was angered, "The sword it will be and to the devil with your dancing!"

The Dark Knight threw back his head and laughed as the prince drew his father's great sword.

"Careful now, boy," he told him, "tis a weighty matter you bring to the day."

"Enough talk," said the prince, "defend yourself."

Again, the Dark Knight laughed, and instead of a sword, he drew from a sheath, a small, bejeweled dagger, and pointed it at the young man,

> *My soul holds no anger*
> *Your bold self I see*
> *The heart that you long for*
> *Already in me*
> *Our purpose is one*
> *Yet one must now die*

*You may find your life's meaning
From the wound to your thigh.*

But the Prince had heard enough. "Defend yourself!" he cried again, lunging forwards.

The Dark Knight avoided the first blow easily, and the prince lunged again, but again the black man spun, evading the great blade without effort.

"Press on young prince," he called out. "Press on if you would, and I will teach you how to dance!"

The young man was infuriated. He was known throughout his father's kingdom as adept with a sword, yet this arrogant stranger was making a mockery of all he knew, displaying none of the respect that was legendary among men of honour. The prince decided to give him no quarter. He slashed at him again, but again the man slipped by the flashing blade, always just slightly out of reach as the prince flailed wildly with the heavy sword.

"Fight back," the prince shouted, "Stand and fight like a man!"

But suddenly the Dark Knight turned, and evading a wild sweep of the prince's sword, he dived in underneath the blade, his dagger flashing in the sunlight like a serpent's tongue.

The prince felt the blow to his groin, yet still he spun, swinging the sword around in a great sweeping arc, slicing through the air, wishing to take the head from this insolent stranger. But his opponent was gone again, ducking and weaving, laughing as if it were nought but a game.

The prince looked down but could see no blood, and he realised that the Dark Knight had struck him with the butt of the dagger, not the blade, and even though his life had been spared he was infuriated.

"Show respect!" The prince screamed. "Fight me like a man, or I will surely have your head!"

He swung the great blade again, but again his opponent was gone, dancing across the meadow as if partaking in some solitary ritual known only to himself. The prince stumbled after him, slashing and thrusting, determined to teach this arrogant trickster the lesson he deserved. He swung at him again and again, but he could feel himself tiring. He thought of his father, and he remembered the old king's words: "You are not yet ready to take the throne." The memory angered him, and once again he tried to swing the great blade, but the sword had grown too heavy in his hands, and he found himself unable to lift the blade. He stumbled and fell then, completely exhausted, and suddenly the Dark Knight was standing above him, dagger raised.

"Yield," the Dark Knight demanded, "Yield or die."

The young man lay there helpless, knowing that his dreams of glory were over, knowing that he would never again return to his father's castle.

"I will never yield," he said, struggling to raise his sword.

The prince saw the flash of the dagger and murmured a prayer. But there was a smashing, ringing sound, and he saw his father's sword high up into the air, turning over and over in the morning sunlight, before plunging down into the lake, and disappearing without trace into the still, dark waters.

"I am no longer armed," the prince felt a spark of hope. "By the rules of combat, I claim my horse and my lance."

"You would challenge me again," said the Knight.

"It is my right," said the prince.

The two men walked their horses to opposite sides of the field. The young man knelt in prayer for a moment, beseeching God to help him destroy this arrogant man so that he might return to his father's house with honour. Then he gathered his lance and shield and remounted Fastus.

As the two men faced each other the prince thought of the warriors he had known, and of the achievements they had won in battle. And he felt a growing rage within him as he stared down the field to where his opponent sat motionless on his horse.

"I will prove myself this day," he whispered, "I will teach this man to respect me."

The Dark Knight and his horse were prancing about at the opposite end of the field, "Are you ready to fight, young man?" he called out.

"Are you ready to die?" called back the Prince.

The two men lowered their visors and without another word gave their horses their heads. Driving their spurs deep into their flanks, the horses charging forward. Stretching out their long, muscled legs, sensing that this was the moment they had trained for all their lives. Thundering towards each other, both beasts' eyes wide, nostrils flaring, gaining momentum with each reaching stride, the earth quaking beneath their thrusting bulk.

They came together in the center of the meadow. The young prince's lance, trained in a hundred tournaments, went straight to the Dark Knight chest. Driving through the scarlet heart emblazoned on the man's armour. The spear tip emerging from his back, reddened by blood. But before the

Dark Knight toppled from his saddle, his lance pierced the prince's armour, wounding the young man in his groin. And as his opponent fell backwards over the rump of his horse, the prince toppled sideways, down onto the thick green grass of the meadow.

They landed side by side, and to his dying day the prince would tell of the Dark Knight's last words.

"The dance!" he'd whispered. "To lead your people, you must know how to dance!"

The old man was refilling his pipe. Pulling the tobacco out from the soft leather pouch with a thumb and forefinger. Packing it into the bowl. Tamping it down smooth and even. Looking up at me occasionally in the quiet of the pause.

"Well, the young prince was a man of honour, and as the fervour of battle waned, it troubled him that the Dark Knight had spared his life only to lose his own. He sat there for some time, his face in his hands, then he went and knelt by the Knight's body and prayed for the man's soul. Then he dug a shallow grave and laid the Dark Knight to rest."

The old man struck a match, and I sat there watching him as he put it to the new pipe.

"After he'd rested for a while, he went in search of his father's sword. He sought for hours in the reeds and then further out in the deeper water, but to no avail. Finally, wounded, and exhausted, he climbed back on Fastus, and began the long journey home.

Days later, as he approached the castle, his father's men, recognising his banner, threw open the gates, rode out to greet him. His father was an old man by then and he was relieved that his son had returned safely for he knew his own days were numbered.

But although he was happy to be home, the young prince remained sick from a wound that refused to heal. Weeks became months, months became years, and still, he could not walk. Healers and mystics were summoned from all over the kingdom, but nothing could be done, and he lay on his bed each day, too wounded to attend to his duties, not sick enough to die."

The old man was staring into the fire, as if seeking out the hidden meaning of the story.

"You see, his father died just a few years later and the prince took the throne. He was in constant pain, holding court whenever he could, lying in his bed when he could not. Some days his men would carry him to a boat, and he'd lay there on cushions fishing. But even when he caught a fish, he was unable to pull it in from the water, and that only served to depress him further. Some tried to find him a consort, but he knew that he could neither love nor be a decent husband to any woman, and so he dissuaded them from their endeavours. Magicians and healers came from far off lands, drawn on by the promise of gold. But despite all that, nothing changed. And as the years passed a despair settled over the kingdom. The cattle became infertile, the crops failed, the rivers ran dry, the politicians quarreled among themselves, and the people lost hope, as the lands fell into poverty and ruin.

But then, one winter's night, after lying restless in his bed for hours, praying for it all to end, he dreamt of the Dark Knight. He dreamt that the Knight was standing in the meadow where they had fought, holding out his father's sword. And the Dark Knight was calling out to him in a loud voice saying, "Whom does the Crown serve?" The dream was so powerful that he rose from his bed and called for his most trusted advisors, and by candlelight he told them of his dream.

"I am called," he told them, "I am called to return once more to the place where I was wounded."

His advisors were alarmed. "Sire," they told him, "You are not fit to travel. And what of the kingdom? Who will rule if you do not return?'

"If I do not return, then my sister, Princess Creaduel will replace me on the throne," he told them. "She is a warrior and a woman of honour, and she will lead the kingdom well. Those are my commands. If I do not return within three months of this day, I forfeit my crown and you will accept Creaduel as your queen."

"But you are loved by your people, your majesty," said one. "You are our king and have no need to do this thing. We will support you. Live out your days here with us, where we will care for you." But the king would not be moved and the next morning he called for his horse and his armour. He had seen in the dream that he rode the same steed as before, but when Fastus was found and brought to him he almost wept, for the old horse had been found at the knacker's yard, awaiting slaughter. And what had once been the pride of the palace stables was now an old nag, feeble and raddled with age. The white of his forequarters discoloured, his shiny black hindquarters faded to grey. But he bade them clean and prepare the horse nevertheless, for this was how it had been in the dream.

When his armour was brought to him the king found that he was too weak to bear it and instead chose simple woolen clothing that weighed but little. They brought him one of his father's old swords, but finding it too heavy, he chose instead a small dagger, curved in the blade.

And that was how he rode out the second time. Late in the afternoon, no fanfare to proceed him, Fastus no longer prancing. No armour, yet comfortable in his woven clothes. No great sword, just a dagger at his belt, to protect himself from thieves. He believed in his mind that he was riding towards death, but he knew in his heart that this was the only honourable thing he could do.

His horse was no longer young, and it was the fifth day before they reached the forest. And there to his surprise, the same old woman sat waiting. He told her,

"I am glad that we meet again
or you've been long on my mind
The words that I used last
Were cruel and unkind
I was young and ambitious
I ask forgiveness dear crone
I now seek the Dark Knight
To surrender my Throne."

The old crone smiled up at him, and her eyes clear and bright,

"There's a change in you, sire
That's plain to see
The Dark Knight awaits you
Though troubled you be
But there are questions to answer

Royal vows to preserve
The question your Majesty
Whom does the crown serve?"

He left her there, and turning Fastus's head to the trees, the King began pushing his way into the forest as before. He found the clearing without effort and, after searching for hours without success for the Dark Knight's grave, he tended to his horse, gathered twigs for his bed, and lay down to rest.

When he awoke, Fastus was standing by the stream, and to the king's surprise, looking as young as he had ever known it to be. The grey of the horse's shoulders had changed overnight and was now a glistening black, while his rump was pure white. He was marveling at these changes when a movement at the far side of the meadow caught his eye and the Dark Knight appeared from the forest once again in all his dark splendour. His great warhorse pawing the ground, his lance glinting in the morning light. His armour and shield relieved only by the scarlet heart emblazoned in the center of the shield.

"You come to do battle once again?" called out the Dark Knight.

"I come to meet you, as in a dream," the king called back.

"Then you come to die the second death."

"I have not slept one full night these past ten years," said the king, "My heart felt your death had no cause."

"Then perhaps it will be your turn to die this day," said the Knight.

"Be that as it may," said the king, "for it is not death I fear, but a life without purpose. I was wounded those many years ago and am of no use to myself nor to my people. I will join you today once more in battle. And if I am to live, then it will be for my people, and if I am to die, then that will set my people free."

"You are prepared to die for your people?" The Dark Knight demanded.

"Yes," said the king. "I will live for them, or I will die for them, whatever God decides. For with me as their leader, they have suffered too long." And at that very moment, the king's wound opened, and the small, pointed tip of the Dark Knight's lance fell out onto the ground, and he was healed. The king reached down unthinkingly, and picking up the tip and there, engraved on the black steel the single word: *Amore*.

And as he looked up, the Dark Knight stepped from his horse and removed his helmet. And to the king's astonishment, there before him stood the most beautiful woman he had ever seen, and he knew at once that she was of royal blood.

The king bowed his head, "I am your servant."

"Then I am your queen," she bowed in return, "And together we shall serve our people."

✧ ✧ ✧

"That's quite a story," I said, "So the king must serve his people, not the other way around."

"When a leader has learnt that their duty is to serve their people, not themselves. When a leader has accepted that part of himself that is feminine and let go of the arrogant side of ego. Only then are they fit to rule. No matter if they be king, queen, taoiseach, prime minister, or president. We must judge our leaders by how they help their people, not by how they help themselves. Not by their words, but by their actions, by how they protect and serve their kingdoms," he rose from the chair, and walked across to the door. "Good night Con Rua," he turned, "Wednesday evening, time for your meeting."

CHAPTER 22

The Priest

WHEN I ARRIVED at the hall, Aiden was setting out chairs, a kettle already steaming on the bench.

"Good evening, Conor. I was given the keys to open up tonight."

"That's great." I said, "How's the head?"

"Ah, not too bad. But it's not easy." He looked like he'd lost a dollar and found a dime. "Two weeks and three days without a drop. I'm thinking of going across to Galway, to see the bishop."

"Why's that, Aiden?"

"Well, he had me sent me over here on leave of absence, for my drinking. But I'm a sober man now, and I want him to know that. I'm off my head now with boredom, and I need to get back to the job."

"Look, you're doing well, but it's probably best if you leave it for a while. A few months of sobriety would impress him a lot more."

"You have no faith in me at all, do ye?"

"It's not that, mate." I told him, "I bust a few times myself before I got sober. I know what it's like."

"So, when does it stop; the craving I mean?"

"When you hit rock bottom and surrender. It's different

for everyone."

"Jaysus, sure am I not at rock bottom now? Coming to these meetings in the middle of the night. Spilling your guts to your own parishioners!"

"Aiden, if you stick with the program, you've got a chance. You've already proven you can't do it alone. And they're not your parishioners, mate, they're recovering alcoholics, the same as yourself."

CHAPTER 23

The Fitzgerald's

WHEN FITZGERALD'S ARRIVED on Inis Mór the following week, I boarded the ferry the moment the gangplank was in place, worried that he might have reneged on our deal. But when I went below, I discovered Dierdre and Cillian sitting in the saloon, surrounded by suitcases.

"Welcome to Inis Mór," I was looking around, "Where's Fitz?"

"He's up above," Dierdre shook her head, "Go up there now and put his mind at ease, Conor."

He was on the upper deck. A wide brimmed hat and sunglasses, scanning the crowd below.

"Fitz," I called out, "is everything okay?"

"I'm fine, Conor, fine," he looked as if there were other places he'd rather be, "There's suitcases and three chests of tools to go ashore, but we'll wait till the crowd thins a little,"

✧ ✧ ✧

WE WERE THE last off the ferry. I'd brought Tessie down with me, so we loaded the heavy chests on the trap and dropped them off outside the boatshed, before we continued on up to my place.

"There's a little cottage over there that might suit you," I pointed it out as we left the quayside, "Three bedrooms, and it's only a hundred yards or so from the boatshed. It belonged to Mrs. Kelly. She died a few years ago and it's been empty since. Her son's lived in America for years, so he's only too happy to rent it out. But it will need a few repairs and a paint job before you move in. It was rethatched just a few years ago so the roof should be sound, although Lorcan thinks there may be a leak somewhere."

"That won't be a problem," Fitz nodded, "We can fix the place up as we go along."

I showed them around my place as soon as we arrived.

"The big bedroom's yours," I told Dierdre, "Cillian can have the other one. I'm happy up above. Have you eaten?"

"We had breakfast at home," Fitz was edgy, "But I need to get back down there and take a look at that boat."

"We'll go together," Dierdre said.

We took the pony and trap back down to the quayside. Fitz still wearing the sunglasses, the hat pulled low.

Tim was sweeping the front steps of the shop as we trotted past.

"Morning Tim."

"Good morning, Con Rua," a big smile, "You're a terrible man, so you are."

I waved, but didn't stop, I didn't want him telegraphing the whole island about our new arrivals. Lorcan was on his knees tending to the fire as we entered the shed. He took a hold of the brick surround and pulled himself to his feet, then approached Fitz, hand outstretched.

"Welcome to Inis Mór, it's a great honour to have a poet of

your standing on this island."

"You know my work?"

"I do indeed, I have two of your books. Would you consider a night of poetry for us here?"

"Meaning what?"

"Well, we have the community hall," Lorcan gestured. "It would be a great way to introduce you to everyone."

Fitz looked across at me, "Was this your idea?"

"No, it never crossed my mind."

He stared at me a moment longer then turned back to Lorcan, "No, I'm sorry. I'm here to fix a boat, nothing more."

"But Fitz," I said, "why not? It would be a good way to meet some of the islanders."

"No, I only do that sort of thing for a few friends occasionally. We have enough on our hands now without poetry."

"We're to be here six months or more, my love," Dierdre was standing by the door with Cillian, "it would be a good way for us to get to know a few of the local people. It's not all about you, you know."

"You should do it, Da," Cillian joined in, "You do it at home, you can do it here."

Fitz stared at his wife, struggling with internal demons. Finally, after a silence that dragged on forever, "All right, but not too many people. One night. Maybe an hour or so at most," he turned back to Lorcan, "When?"

"Well, we normally we do plays and things like that in the big hall on a Sunday evening. That's four days from now."

"Fine," Fitz nodded, "Sunday it is."

CHAPTER 24

Poetry

THE NEXT FEW days were chaotic. Organizing the boatshed, setting up equipment. Bolting the big circular saw to the heavy wooden bench. Adjusting *Aman Cara's* cradle. Writing out endless lists of what was needed. Timber, brass deck fittings, bronze castings, galvanized rigging, all carried out under Fitz's perfectionist eye.

But it soon became obvious that Fitz was regretting the poetry night, for the tension around him was palpable. Barking out orders, snapping at Cillian, ignoring my questions.

"Look, Fitz," I took him aside, "If the poetry thing is messing with your head, we can cancel it. There's still time."

He was working on the fuse box, running new leads up the wall and across the rafters. Fitting overhead lights that would shine directly down on *Aman Cara*.

"You go about your own business now, Conor," he didn't look up, "and leave me to mine."

"Okay," I said, "Is there anything you need?"

"Yes, go up above and get me my screwdrivers. They were left in a leather pouch on the bench in the kitchen. After that you'd be well advised to leave me alone."

I left him there stewing and rode my bike home, Dierdre's

voice and the strains of her harp greeting me as I approached the cottage. She was sitting with her back to me, just outside the kitchen door. A shawl over her shoulders, her fingers moving across the chords. A small group of seagulls listening, heads tilted, on the stone path in front of her. I tiptoed in quietly, but the birds startled, and she turned.

"You're home."

"Yes, there's nothing much I can do down there and your man's in a mood."

She burst out laughing and put aside the harp.

"Don't worry about Fitz, he'll settle down. It will take time; he's nervous with strangers."

"He can't hide in the shed forever, Dierdre."

"Con, you know what happened. That woman broke his heart. How would you be having to look at that face in the mirror every morning?"

"That's a bit harsh," I said, "and that's what you see every morning."

"No, I don't. We don't see faces; we only see hearts."

"Who's we?" I asked.

"My own kind," she flicked her head, brushing off my question, "I have known many hearts, but none like his. He spent his young life caring for his father. His father was a broken man after he lost his wife that way. He couldn't look after himself, let alone Fitz. Fitz had to look after him. The same way he looks after myself and our boy. That fierceness he hides behind is just a mask. He's still a frightened little boy at heart, hoping that the world will look at him one day without flinching."

"And you think being here might help him?"

"It may, for he now has the chance to stand up to the demons that have haunted him these past many years."

"And you're sure he can do that?"

"No, I'm not. He will either rise or fall on Inis Mór."

"And if he falls, what then?"

"Then, we'll either start over again in Galway, or go our separate ways."

"You'd leave him?"

"Conor, I love him. But a husband with half a heart is no good to man nor beast. He must learn to face his fears and stop hiding."

"You mean by accepting himself?"

"By understanding that we are all dealt a hand in this life, and our job is to play that hand as best we can. Some come into this world handsome or beautiful, some not. Others worry because they believe they are too fat or too thin. Some believe they're too tall or too short, the list is endless. You must start by realizing that you are unique, yet one with all mankind. That your appearance does not matter one bit. It is what you do with your life that counts. That is what sets us free. By letting go of fear and finding a way to give something back to this world. By becoming the person we were born to be."

"Where are you from?" It was out before I could stop it.

"Why do you ask?"

"I just wondered," I said, "You're so different."

"You should ask Fitz."

CHAPTER 25

Second Thoughts

FITZ CHANGED HIS mind a dozen times that day, moving the big work bench from one side of the shed to the other, then back again. Tearing out the wiring he'd just installed and starting over from scratch. Levelling and releveling *Anam Cara*. Stalking out of the shed at times to stand at the far end of the jetty, as if considering diving in and swimming back to Galway. Then striding back to check out the community hall one more time. Now he was back.

"I won't be reciting any poems in that hall tonight, they have a hundred seats in there and the place lit up like a carnival," he was fuming. "I need the lights dimmed, same as Galway. No, we'll be doing it here in the boatshed, do you hear me? Go over there now and tell him the same."

"Are you sure?" I said, "They're nearly finished setting up."

"Go over there now and tell them it's either here, or not at all, up to you." I went across to the hall.

✧ ✧ ✧

"BUT WE'RE ALMOST done," Lorcan was baffled.

"It's the boatshed or nothing," I told him, "If you want to argue with him, he's over there now."

They spent the next two hours ferrying chairs and tables across to the shed. Fitz had left by then, so I followed him back to my place.

When I arrived, he was out in the backyard. Arms folded tightly across a barrel chest. Staring out across the ocean, as if willing himself to be anywhere but Inis Mór. Dierdre watching from the kitchen.

"I'm sorry, Conor," she turned, "He's changed his mind. He won't be there tonight. You must go back down there now and tell them."

"Jesus, Dierdre, half the island's coming! Should I try talking to him?"

"No, nothing will shake him now. That woman has him banjaxed. Go below and tell them maybe another time."

"Tell them I'm not well," Fitz was by the door, "and that's close to the truth. I was a fool to agree in the first place. Every time I walk down that road, I'm stared at as if I'm something escaped from a freak show! And Conor, we'll be moving into Mrs. Kelly's cottage tomorrow."

"You can't live there yet," I told him, "The roofs not fixed and there's a storm forecast!"

"We're moving in tomorrow. I'll have the roof fixed in a day or two, the rest as we go along. It's close to the boatshed and it's private, and that's what I need,"

"You can't hide on a small island like this, Fitz."

"I'm here to rebuild a boat, Conor. That, and nothing more. I don't need the islanders, and they don't need me; okay? As soon as the job's done, we'll be off back home."

His face was set like stone, so I rode back down to the

boatshed and broke the news to Lorcan.

"But why?"

"I don't know, you've seen him, he's just shy, I guess."

CHAPTER 26

Integrity

THEY MOVED OUT of my place the following morning, carrying everything down to Mrs. Kelly's place in the pony and trap, and for the next few days I hardly saw them. Fitz called in occasionally, to pick up timber or tools, then he'd be gone again, just as quick.

"How's it going over there," I asked, "Have you fixed the leak?"

"Yes, the roof's done. The wind had one corner lifted. I had that fixed in no time. I'll be working on *Anam Cara* before the week's out."

"No rush," I told him, "Just make sure the cottage is right."

✧ ✧ ✧

I WORKED LATE that evening, preparing, then revarnishing the bulkheads in *Erin's* cabin. And when I heard someone moving about below, I assumed that Fitz had returned. But when I stuck my head out of the hatch, the old man was standing by the fire in his overcoat, hands stretched out to the flames.

"The weather's fierce out there," he smiled up at me, "It's to be expected this time of the year."

"Fitz was here earlier," I climbed down to join him, "He

was hoping to catch up with you."

"Ah, Fitz. He's a bit of a lad that one."

"He's all of that," I said.

I put the kettle on and watched the old man as he walked around *Anam Cara*. Examining the damage, inspecting the broken ribs, examining the bronze fittings Fitz had brought over from Galway. Running his fingers over a wood carving, Cillian had left on the big bench.

"This is his boy's work?"

"Yes, he's obsessed with carving."

"Take note of the quality, Con Rua. What you're calling an obsession, is clearly a passion," he shook his head, "Don't ever confuse the two. Obsessions are based on the self, the ego, greed. True passion comes from the heart, empowered by the gift of purpose."

"Purpose?"

"Yes, purpose. The meaning behind the work, the spirit, the intent. Why do you do things? Is it just for yourself, or will it benefit others too? If you're obsessed with something trivial or mundane, it's invariably for yourself. If you are pursing your true purpose with passion, then you're offering something back to your family, and to the world."

"You mean like an artist or a sculptor?"

"Yes, but not everyone can be an artist. People are called to a hundred different vocations. The dedicated schoolteacher, the builder who builds with pride, the doctors who truly care for their patients. If the poets, priests, or politicians are passionate in their work, then they are fulfilling their true purpose in life. All using the gifts they were given, all making the world a better place, yet none of them demanding fame or fortune, for the reward lies in the giving."

I handed him a mug of tea and watched as he settled back in his chair.

"And Fitz's boy is doing that?"

"Of course," he looked up, "and your boy? Does he not have dreams of his own?"

"No, Tristan has no idea what he wants to do," I told him, "We talked about it in Brittany."

"And how could you expect him to have any dreams?"

"How do you mean?"

"Well, he never had a guide. You were never there for him. You said as much yourself."

I felt a surge of anger, "I'm here for him now," I told him, "And, like I said, we talked about it in Brittany."

"Children don't learn by talking, Conor. They learn by watching and observing. That's where you went wrong, for you had no father to guide you."

The wind was beginning to howl outside, rattling the iron sheeting on the roof, blowing smoke back down the chimney in the stronger gusts.

"But I've changed," I said, "Give me some credit for that!"

There was a long silence as he stared across at me.

"Well, you're thinking may have changed," he conceded, "I'll give you that. But it takes time for new beliefs to become part of who you are," he took a draw on the pipe, "You see, boy, you've had gremlins living in your head for years. *They are in you as you*, and they won't be leaving without a fight."

"*In me as me?*" I said, "What does that mean?"

"It means all your old ideas and imaginings. All the things that were instilled in your mind as a child. All the false notions you've taken on board yourself. Your prejudices, biases, and beliefs. Notions that may well have helped you survive in your younger days but work against you now. Everything that you consider to be *you*. All the things you unconsciously refer to when you say *I, or me. They are in you, as you, but they are not you.*"

"So, who am I then?"

A roll of thunder drowned out the question, so I said again, "So, who am I?"

"You are simply a person, a person like any other. A person with the same abilities that most other people have. A person who came to believe certain things and behave in certain ways. You can't think your way out of that. *New values must be lived if they are to become an integral part of you and what you are.*"

"And how do you do that?"

"That's easy answered. One day at a time. One kept promise at a time, one truthful statement, one honest deed, one selfless act. That, repeated faithfully, day after day, will begin to displace all of your old ideas and delusions. But you don't fight those delusions, understand? You just let them go. Then your new beliefs and values will begin to take root and grow. Until they in turn become *in you, as you.*"

"How long does all that take?"

"It will take as long as it takes. But if you are committed, you will begin to see and feel the changes within weeks."

"So, is Fitz in the same boat as me?"

"No!" He threw back his head and laughed, "Oh, no, Fitz and yourself are black and white. You were the handsome one in the fancy car, dashing out into the world. Expensive suits and ties. The flashing smiles. Hail fellow well met. The man who presented well yet couldn't look after his own family. Fitz is the opposite. Secretive. Afraid of the world. Ashamed of his appearance. His body a prison from which he can see no escape, yet a man devoted to his wife and child. A man who would protect them with his life. A man who believed he had no acceptable outside. While you, on the other hand, had no acceptable inside. You came to believe that there was something wrong with you, that you are not enough. Like I said. You're twins you two, shadow images of each other, both halfway along the road to redemption."

He stood and picked up his cane.

"It's pouring down out there," I told him, "Why not wait for a break in the weather?"

He just nodded, smiled, and headed for the door.

CHAPTER 27

Gale Force 6

I WAS IN bed by nine the following evening, it was one of those nights. Gales had been raging around the islands for days, buffeting the doors and windows, tugging at the thatch roof. I read for a while, cocooned within heavy blankets, oblivious to the elements raging just outside the glass panes, before slipping away into a deep sleep.

I was jerked awake at two am, a car's headlights across the bedroom ceiling, raised voices, someone pounding on the door. I pulled on a pair of jeans and ran downstairs.

"There's a yacht in trouble off the coast," Cormac Rafferty, the skipper of the Inis Mór lifeboat and Fitz, were huddled outside in yellow oilskins, rain streaming down their faces, "Three people on board, and we're two men short on the lifeboat. Most of the crew are over in Galway at a wedding. There's a husband, wife, and child on board, we're the only hope they have. Karl's getting the boat into the water as we speak. Are you up for it?"

I ran upstairs, dressed, grabbed my oilskins, then back down, and moments later we were in the truck, racing towards the quay. The tractor was reversing the boat down the ramp as we arrived, and as soon as she was in the water, we boarded her. Karl leaping on board at the very last moment. It was relatively calm in the shelter of the harbour, but the moment we cleared the harbour walls, the full force of the gale hit us.

"Force five, gusting six," the skipper was yelling in my ear, "You and Fitz will be responsible for getting lines to them when we come alongside. Karl will fill you in." He turned, "Karl you're second to me tonight. You know the drill. We'll approach from windward, then work our way down alongside her. Hopefully that will give them enough cover to get on aboard."

The lifeboat was rising and falling like a wild horse, plunging about in the rolling swells. Water surging over her bow and sweeping along the full length of her decks. Five of us huddled in the cabin, squinting through rain-streaked windows.

"How big is she?" Fitz was preparing lifejackets.

"Thirty-three feet I believe," the skipper was fighting with the wheel, struggling to keep her on course. "She's French, out of Marseille. Christ knows what they're doing out on a night like this!"

The noise of the engines was fluctuating wildly. First, we were bow up as we cut into a swell, the engine slowing in the deeper water. Then bow down as the wave passed, the propellers threshing in the aerated foam. Still, she forged ahead steadily, smashing into the waves like a steel bull, wind and rain battering the heavy plate glass windows, the crew gripping on to guardrails with both hands as she tossed like a cork in the raging seas.

"There she is!" The skipper was pointing through the rain-washed glass.

A flare had risen a mile or two off our starboard bow, exploding high above a coal black ocean, illuminating the tumultuous scene below. For a brief moment, I caught a glimpse of the yacht. Way too low in the ocean, her mast down and over the side, dragging her sails and rigging through the water as she drifted helplessly toward a rocky shore.

"She'll not last long by the look of her," Cormac was fighting with the wheel, "Con, be ready with those lines. And, Fitz, have the webbing ready, if they go into the water, it could be their only hope."

We were closing on the stricken vessel. A man waving a torch on the stern, a woman with an arm around a young boy, the other around a guardrail. Me and Fitz out on deck as we closed on the yacht. The man waving. The woman clinging on to the boy.

"Jaysus, they don't have lifejackets!"

We were within yards of them now. Close enough to see the terror on the woman's face. We came alongside and almost touched, but a wave hit us, and we were dragged apart again. The skipper revving the engines, battling with wind and currents, trying to draw close enough to shield them from the worst of the onrushing waves to give them a chance to abandon ship.

Then a monstrous wave rose out of nowhere, slamming us into the side of the wallowing yacht. The impact took the man off his feet, and he fell, smashing his head against the side of our steel hull. Fitz grabbed his lifeless body by the collar and dragged him on board, as the boats were pulled apart again. The woman reaching out a hand, as if willing it to stop it all happening. Cormac revving the engines, seeking another chance to close with the doomed vessel, bellowing through the loudspeaker,

"Be ready to jump! Hold on to that boy! Be ready!" Then as we aligned again, "Now! Jump! Jump!"

The mother grabbed the boy's arm as we came alongside and took a wild leap. But the boy pulled back at the last moment and was torn from her grasp. He fell down into the water and was swept away by the waves.

Fitz snatched at the woman's hair, then her coat, dragging her on board like a broken doll, before carrying her inside to safety.

"Coming about!" the skipper was yelling, "Coming about!" but as he spun the wheel and revved the engines, there was a grinding, shrieking noise and both engines died.

"Props fouled!" He screamed out. "We've lost him."

I rushed to the back of the boat, but it was hopeless. The boy was already a hundred yards away. I grabbed a life raft, pulled the pin, and as it began to inflate, I hurled it as far out as I could in the boy's direction.

Then suddenly Fitz's face was in mine, gripping my head in both hands, a mad look in his eyes, screaming above the roar of the wind and water, "Do not let Dierdre near the sea, Conor. Do you hear me? Do not let her near the water."

And then he was gone, over the side, his great arms flailing, the soles of his bare feet thrashing about behind him, his body moving through the water like some demented sea creature, and within moments he'd disappeared, downwind into the darkness.

"Back to the cabin," the skipper was bellowing over the loud hailer, "All hands back into the cabin, now!"

Cormac was tugging on a black wet suit as we entered,

"I'm going over the side. We have to free those props. Karl, you and Conor take over, and get your safety harnesses on. I'll not lose any more men this night."

"You can't," Karl protested, "It's bloody suicide."

"Follow orders, Karl! We trained for this, and we'll be on those rocks before morning if I don't," he was strapping a toolbelt around his waist, "If I can free the propellers, we still have a chance to save them."

We followed him out, securing his safety harness, double checking the ropes, getting him over the stern. The wind was rising, the boat jerking this way and that as each new wave hit us, lightening flashing overhead.

He was down so long the first time, I thought we'd lost him, then suddenly he was back, hanging onto the stern ladder, gasping for air. A moment later he was back down again, his long black flippers threshing about behind him. The fourth time he came up, he gave us a thumbs up and we dragged him aboard and rushed him back to the wheelhouse, shivering and blue in the face.

"Kick her over, Karl," he was sitting on the floor, shrouded in blankets, "Put her in reverse as soon as you can. Not too hard now." There was a shudder and a muffled roar as the engines came back to life. "Easy now, steady as you go, wait till we clear the ropes."

"The yacht's going down, skipper," Karl called out, "and she's taking the rigging with her."

"Full reverse till I say, then come about in search mode." The skipper was back on his feet, still shaking like a leaf, "I'll need our exact position when they went over the side. We'll circle downwind from there. There's still a chance we can save them,"

We circled for hours. The winds were abating but the seas were still high and by five am our fuel was almost done. We stood together in the cabin, holding hands in prayer. The mother sobbing helplessly, her husband unconscious on the floor as we came about and altered course for Cill Rónáin.

There were only a handful of people on the quay as we arrived, most of the islanders were still sleeping, unaware of the tragedy. The French woman and her husband were rushed up to the doctor's house. A woman from the local radio station was talking to Cormac, holding a microphone in his face.

"He's gone," I told Lorcan, "Fitz is gone. He went over the side trying to rescue a boy."

Then I broke down. Standing with my face in my hands, sobbing like a child.

"You can't blame yourself, Conor," Mary was in bits too, "There's nothing could be done."

"I brought him here…"

"Conor," Lorcan had a hand on my shoulder, "his wife has to be told."

"No," Mary said, "She'll need a woman with her."

"She's not to go near the sea," I told them.

"What?"

"That's what he told me. Just before he went over the side. Fitz grabbed me and said, she's not to go near the sea. He said it twice."

"God almighty!" Mary was staring at Lorcan. "He knew!"

"Knew what?"

"I'm sorry, Conor," Mary was dabbing at her eyes, "But there's been rumors," she shook her head, "She's so different."

"Never mind that old nonsense," Lorcan snapped, "I'm going up there now. Whatever she is, she has to be told."

"No, you stay here," Mary was firm, "She'll need a woman with her,"

"I'll come with you," I said, "I brought him here."

We walked across to Fitz's place, not a word between us.

"I'll do the talking," I told her.

Cillian appeared first, then Dierdre behind, "Is Fitz not with you?" she didn't wait for an answer, "Come in the two of ye', you must be frozen with the cold." We followed her in. There was a fire in the grate, a smell of toast, "Will you have tea or coffee?"

"Coffee," I said.

She swept back out into the kitchen.

"You have to tell her!" Mary was staring at me, wide eyed.

"I know!" I whispered, "I will!"

"There now," she was back, putting a tray down on the table.

"Dierdre…" I began, but suddenly the door flew open and Tim came rushing in.

"He's alive, Dierdre! It just come over the radio. Fitz is alive, and the boy too. The helicopter spotted them on the beach on Inis Meáin. They're both alive and well. The nurse over there's looking after the boy, but Fitz is on his way back in the helicopter! The word's out, people are gathering down on the quay."

CHAPTER 28

Lazarus

As we rushed back down to the quay, a roar came up from the crowd as the helicopter was sighted. It descended slowly into the car park, then the doors opened, and Fitz appeared, swathed in blankets. The moment his feet touched the ground he was hoisted up on men's shoulders, carried up to the boatshed, and put in a chair by the fire. People crowding around. Women bringing hot food and drink. The fishermen demanding to know how he survived.

"Will you leave him be!" Dierdre pushed her way through carrying a mug of tea. "Can you not see he's done in! Get that fire going right for God's sake!"

Within minutes the shed was packed with people. The islanders crowding around. Fitz still smothered in blankets. Dierdre fending off questions. Youngsters staring in the windows, wanting to be part of it all.

As soon as he'd eaten, the questions began again, everyone demanding to know what had happened. Dierdre whispering with him for a moment before moving to the center of the room and holding up her hands.

"Fitz tells me that he needs to apologize to you all for cancelling the poetry evening the other night. He still doesn't feel right about that. He'll never admit it, but he's a shy little thing at heart," a ripple of laughter, "but he's feeling stronger now, and he's ready to tell you what happened out there last night."

There was applause and a few cheers as Fitz settled back in his chair. He paused for a long moment, collecting his thoughts, then began. He told them of how he was awakened by the skipper looking for volunteers. Then he spoke of the severity of the storm, and how it affected him seeing the young boy clinging on to his mother on the doomed yacht.

"I've known that feeling," he told them, "To be lost, I mean. And when that young lad went into the water it was need that took me over the side. For I knew in my heart if I hadn't gone in after him, I could not have lived another moment myself." He paused, rubbing his fingers into his forehead, "People are after telling me I'm a hero; but that's not true. Something takes a hold of ye'. You don't think. I'm sure if you did, you wouldn't go in at all. No, something takes you," he paused, "It's as if you're connected to the other person somehow. As if you're one with them, or as if they're a part of you. Or as if that's you in the water or," he paused again, shaking his head, "as if that's all of us in the water, and we must all decide whether we're going in or not," he shook his head, "I'm not at all sure of what I'm talking about now."

But a murmur ran through the crowd, and it was clear they did.

"I was fortunate. I saw him ahead of me and stuck out towards him. Someone had thrown an inflatable raft into the water and the moment I reached the boy it came by me. Well, by the grace of God I caught a hold of a rope trailing from it. But for that I wouldn't be here at all. The young lad was all but done in by then."

"But the cold," one of the fishermen called out, "did it not stop your heart?"

"Not that I know of," Fitz smiled, "but I'll have Dierdre check as soon as we're home."

There was a burst of laughter, people shouting out comments.

"Stop!" Cormac was on his feet, "Will you let the man finish the story."

"But no," Fitz continued, "I was fine. I got myself up into the raft and dragged the lad up with me. As luck would have it, the current took us close to Inis Meáin. There was a paddle in the boat, and I pulled like mad for the beach. Well, as soon as I saw sand churning in the water I went over the side and dragged the raft in behind me. The boy was unconscious by then, so I carried him ashore. There were lights in a cottage nearby, and I took him up there. The fisherman's wife took over then and within an hour she had him sitting up eating soup."

"You're a hard man, Fitzgerald," one of the fishermen called out.

"I'm here by the grace of God," Fitz shook his head, "The same as the rest of us."

"So, will you be writing a poem about this?" a woman asked.

"I will I suppose, but these things need to settle in me before the words come."

"And you'll recite it for us here at the shed here, will you not?"

"I will, and this time I won't be cancelling on you!"

There was a lot clapping then, the islanders crowding

around Fitz. Men shaking his hand, women hugging him, Dierdre whispering in his ear.

"Now," she turned to face the group, "He's all but done in, so I'm taking him home. But you're all invited to a night of poetry, next Sunday evening, six o'clock, here in the shed."

CHAPTER 29

Sunday

WE ARRIVED AT the boatshed Sunday evening just before five. A few of the islanders were already there, talking in small groups. Men in their Sunday best, ill-fitting black suits, and white shirts. Women in coats and shawls against a biting evening breeze.

We closed the doors behind us to make final preparations. The shed was filled with chairs, sorted by local volunteers. Fitz had become an overnight celebrity and there were people from all over the Aran Islands waiting as I opened the doors at five thirty. Tim and his wife first in the door.

"Con Rua, I'd like you to meet my good wife," then turning to her, "I've told you about Conor, dear, he's the son of Con Rua O'Rourke the seanachaí."

She held out a hesitant hand.

"Now he's not the one who'd have us divorced, is he?"

"Oh, God no!" Tim looked shocked, "Sure Conor's a fierce Catholic altogether. No darling, that was some mad Englishman I was after talking to off the ferry one day. A heathen he was I believe, by the look of him."

People were flowing in, chairs filling quickly, and by six o'clock, it was clear there would be standing room only. It was time to begin.

Lorcan began by telling them that Fitz's wife would give them a song before her husband began, and as he finished the introduction, I took my place at the lighting console.

A few of the young islanders had climbed up on *Anam Cara* and were sitting on her decks, feet dangling over the side. The shed was almost completely dark, a single, soft light partially illuminating a figure sitting in the center of the circle.

As the first notes of the harp rang out, the crowd fell silent. And as I raised the light above Dierdre slowly, one could sense a shift in energy as the islanders stared. She was wearing the same green dress as before, the satin folds falling gently to her bare feet, her long dark hair flowing like waves over one shoulder, her hands moving softly among the chords, her face calm and serene.

Then she began, singing in Irish. Her lilting tones carrying to every corner of the room. People leaning forwards in their chairs. Me still concerned as to whether Fitz would be appearing or not.

At the end of the song, she stood, bowed, and introduced her husband. Then, as I dimmed the lights lower, she joined me by the controls.

Nothing happened for a full minute, and we both sat there motionless. But then I saw him, moving slowly from the shadows, out into the center of the circle.

Dierdre was clinging onto my arm, her fingers digging in so hard I almost pulled away. But then Fitz began, speaking in Irish, his voice firm and clear.

"What's he saying," I asked.

"He's telling them what happened," she said, "about the accident," she paused, "Now he's telling them about how he came to Inis Mór to meet a young woman," she paused again, listening, "He's telling them everything, Conor."

Then Fitz turned to where we were sitting.

"The lights," he called out in English, "Raise up the lights, Con Rua," I did, "More," he shouted, "Go on, Con, higher, higher." I pushed the lever over to full power.

"That's it, Fitz," I shouted back, "that's full power," It was, the overhead globes flooding the shed with light, illuminating every corner of the room. Fitz standing there like a pirate, hands on hips, head thrown back, a broad smile denying his distorted features, his eyes bright and alive as he stared back at the islanders. Dierdre on her feet, tears in her eyes.

He stood there for a long moment, then he said: "*Sinn e mise*," before turning and sitting down in the captain's chair.

"What did he say?" I asked her, "Just then, what did he say?"

There were tears on her cheeks, "He said, *Sinn e mise*. This am I."

✧ ✧ ✧

I SOFTENED THE lights as he began, not understanding a word he was saying, but captivated by the lilting tones and inflections of his voice. The words touching some ancient memory of race, and home, and blood. The guttural intonations of the language touching years of denial in my soul, bringing both tears and joy to my heart.

The first poem was lengthy, and by the timber of his voice, sad, and before he was halfway through women were dabbing at their eyes with handkerchiefs. This was followed by a poem that altered the mood immediately. The words staccato and abrupt, the laughter beginning by the second verse. Dierdre clasping her hands like a child. The islanders taken with laughter. It was clear he had them entranced.

The session was slated to wrap up by eight pm, but the calls to continue were so persistent, Fitz was still in the chair an hour later. When he finally rose, we all stood, thinking it was over, but then he announced in English that there was a surprise guest.

"Who could that be?" I asked Dierdre.

Before she could answer he was speaking again.

"Now, some of us knew the late Con Rua O'Rourke, the Seanachaí of Inis Mór. Well, please welcome his son, Conor O'Rourke, here to tell you a story of his own…"

I was stunned, and I sat there frozen, my mind racing.

"Get up," Dierdre whispered, "Tell them a story."

They were all staring at me, waiting.

"I'm sorry," I stood up, "I don't have a story ready for tonight, maybe another time."

"Tell us the story about the selkie," Brigid O'Neil was sitting in the front row, an impish grin on her face, "the one Lorcan told you. Tell us that one, if you will."

"Come on now, Conor," Fitz was enjoying himself, "you said yourself that the gift was an obligation. Come down here now and tell us a story."

"Go on," Dierdre's voice in my ear, "Go down and surprise us all."

I stood, my brain reeling. I was trapped.

"Speak from your heart," Fitz whispered as I arrived by his side, "whatever story comes to mind, speak from your heart."

I turned to face them. "Look, I'm sorry," I told them, "There is a story I heard in Brittany. But I don't have it ready for you tonight."

There was silence for a long moment.

"Will you have it ready by Christmas Eve?" Brigid called out.

"Yes," I said, "I believe so."

"Well, there you have it," Dierdre had an arm around me, "We have another shy one on our hands," there was a ripple of laughter, "But we have a promise for Christmas Eve, which is better than nothing at all!"

CHAPTER 30

Denial

I DIDN'T SLEEP that night. Images of Fitz and his wife haunting me. The way he'd held the room, his words flowing in endless streams. And Dierdre, graceful as a swan, stroking the chords of the harp, head thrown back, the islanders sitting there entranced.

And I realized that I envied them. Not so much for what they had, but for what I lacked.

Maybe this storytelling is all bullshit, I told myself. *The important thing is that I have a job and I can support my wife. Maybe the seanachaí stuff can come later, after we get on our feet.*

But some internal bell chimed *no*. A bell I knew only too well. I got out of bed, showered, shaved, and took a coffee out to my perch in the backyard.

Maybe I don't want to be a seanachaí. Maybe I should just write stories, or articles for magazines. Maybe a book later on. But again, that bell. It always happened when I was making excuses for something that I knew I should do. An off note, like some distant graveyard bell, warning me that I should stop, think, and be honest with myself.

Reason told me that none of that made any sense, but by now I knew that my soul held a purpose that reason knew little of.

CHAPTER 31

The Cycles of Life

I ARRIVED AT the boatshed late Monday morning, my breath preceding me like puffs of steam in the cold air. My leather bomber jacket doing little to save me from a bitter wind coursing in across a bleak, wave tossed Atlantic.

Entering through the wicket gate, I was relieved to see that the shed had been tidied. Chairs stacked, tables folded, leftover food wrapped in paper. I put the kettle on, set a fire, then built it up with logs. I was still on my knees fanning the flames when Fitz arrived.

"There's left over sandwiches there," I told him, "And the kettles on."

"She was there last night you know, Rebecca," he was arranging mugs on the bench.

"I wondered. I saw you talking to a red-haired woman by the door."

"Yes, that was her."

He was pouring water into the teapot, steam swirling around him.

"How did it go?"

"Well, I told her that she was as beautiful as the first day I laid eyes on her, but then I said I was sorry, but we couldn't marry now as I was already taken."

"You did not!"

"I did so. Then I explained to her that I had to take back a piece of my heart from her so as to return it to my wife."

"Did she understand that?"

"I'm not sure, but she introduced me to her husband, and we ended up laughing together, so I'm free of it now."

He brought a mug of tea over and I passed him a plate of sandwiches.

"How are things at the cottage?" I asked.

"It's going well. I'm here to pick up a few tools. The front door's fixed, but the window frames are in bad shape, and there's a couple of floorboards that need to be replaced. After that there's only the paint left, and Dierdre and Cillian are looking after that. Another few days I'll be ready to back work here."

"Great. I called Galway last night and put an order in with Gwen. When I told her you'd moved into Mrs. Kelly's place, she said Patrick would be happy to pay the rent."

"Tell her thank you but no," he bit into a sandwich, "I'll be paying my own rent, Conor. I'll not be the cottage cat."

"She said we can order all the timber precut from Galway."

"No, I cut my own wood." he turned, "There are some nice baulks of oak over there in the woodpile, and some good lengths of larch too. The oak will do fine for her hull, we'll use the larch above," he paused, "Now, Con, we need to get things straight between the two of us. You're in charge of this project, I accept that. But as you said you're an amateur, and I'll not be accountable to any man for my work."

"I know that" I told him, "Patrick asked that I make sure everything's done right, that's my main role here. The way I see it; you're the boatbuilder, I'm the apprentice."

"Good, we understand each other so," we shook hands, "Now, once we start, I'll be pulling out whatever needs to be fixed. A few of her ribs will have to be replaced. That's a two-man job, and I'll need your help with the planking and some of the heavier work too."

"Okay, I'll be here when you need me. When you don't, I'll work on her fastenings and stuff like that. You want all the fastenings checked, right?"

"Yes, every one. It will take time, but it must be done. Later we'll be steaming planks, have you done that before?"

"Yes, I steamed all the planks for *Erin*."

✧ ✧ ✧

AFTER FITZ LEFT, I returned to *Erin*, and began scraping weed and barnacles off her hull. It was slow, tedious work, and I was happy to pause for a break when the old man appeared through the door late in the afternoon.

"Good evening," I was always struck by the formality of his greetings.

"Good evening," I said, "You missed Fitz, he was here earlier."

"He did well last night," he smiled.

"You were there?"

He was walking around *Erin*, inspecting her hull, picking at strands of caulking that were bulging from seams in her planking, "These will need to be addressed," he said, "It's not a big job but it must be done right,"

"I know, I'm going to pull the loose stuff out later, then I'll redo the caulking. Can I offer you tea?"

"Thank you."

He was warming himself by the fire as I put on the kettle.

"There's cake there," I said.

"Thank you," he sat down, "just the tea will be fine."

"You look worried," I handed him a mug, "Is there something wrong?"

He stared at me for a long moment.

"I'll not be here forever, Con Rua, and there are things you must know."

"Like what?" I said.

"What is your understanding of the triskele?"

"It's an ancient Celtic symbol. It's on the top of the walking stick you gave me. You said it was the sign of the seanachaí."

"Yes, among other things. The seanachaí did use the triskele in their teaching,"

"Teaching, or storytelling?"

"There is teaching enshrined in every good story," he took out his pipe, "The Celts have used storytelling throughout the ages to convey knowledge. You can't teach people by just telling them things. There's many a mind that rebels against lectures, boy. But if the message is offered from the heart, other hearts will open to it. Christ, the Budha, Plato, the High Priestess Pythia, the Oracle at Delphi, they all spoke in parables. Stories are a pathway to the soul, therein lies their power."

"And the triskele," I asked, "how does that fit in?"

He reached for his cane, "See here," he showed me the symbol embedded in the head of his walking stick. Fine silver filigree embedded in a gold surround. "There are three circles.

The three stages of life. And in the very center, a small circle," he looked up at me, "That inner circle represents the Life Force, God if you will. The supreme power that infuses all of life. From the tiniest amoeba crawling along through the primordial ooze, to the power demonstrated by the prophets, mystics, and all the other great spiritual leaders that came to this world to raise the consciousness of mankind." His eyes were bright, "That is the power that gives us the energy needed to follow our purpose in life."

"Why are you telling me this?"

"I will not be here forever, and this knowledge must be passed on." he raised his eyes, "Just two years ago you yourself were living in a delusory world. Convinced you were a big shot. Obsessed with material possessions. Drinking, drugs, running around Sydney, full of ego. Trying to impress others whilst ignoring the needs of your own family." We stared at each other, "And at the time you considered that to be a normal life. You were trapped in a delusion. A very common delusion in today's world. Living in a fantasy land with no understanding of who or what you were."

"Go on," I said.

"Then you had voices in your mind telling you that you were wasting your life. Voices calling on you to change. You accepted that call when you asked for help,"

"I've changed a lot since then," I told him.

"Yes, you've had a good look at yourself, and you now have a better idea of who you are. You've accepted your responsibilities as a husband and father, you have a job, and you've discovered your gift," he paused and smiled for the first time, "So, you have completed the various stages of the first circle.

Something we all of us must do if we are to live authentic lives."

"So, the first step is examining who and what we are right now, yes?"

"Yes. In the first stage you examine where you stand in the world. And you must be honest with yourself. Is your life enriched by family and friends? Are you wanted, needed, and loved, by your actions? Are you fulfilled in your work? Does your life hold meaning? If you come up lacking in these areas, then you must ask yourself why," he smiled, "You see, until you know what your purpose is in life, you're a ship without a destination, a boat without a rudder."

"And I've completed the first circle?"

"You had the first circle done before you left for Brittany."

"So, I move on to the second circle, yes?"

"Yes. The ancients called the first circle *The Unconscious Life*, the second circle is known as *Becoming*. This is when your destiny becomes clearer. And by this stage you know, or at least you suspect, that there is a power in this world that will help and guide you, just so long as you stay true to your heart."

"You mean, God?" I asked.

"Most call it God. Myself, I'm comfortable with the ancient Irish term, the Life Force. That, to me, embraces all beliefs, without the need to disagree or argue with anyone."

"So, I'm ready to move into the second circle?"

"You have already entered the second circle. The challenge for you now is to find a way to offer that gift back to the world in such a way that will benefit both yourself and others."

"I'm pretty happy with the way things are at the moment," I told him, "All I need now is for my family to rejoin me."

"But it's not so much about you, as your gift," he looked

across at me, "The true seanachaí offer knowledge to their listeners. Stories that will enthuse and inspire them to help their families, their communities, and ultimately the world itself. You have that gift, Con Rua, that is why you were chosen."

"Chosen for what?"

"I am old;" he stared at me, shadows flickering like grief in his eyes, "You are young. You are the future; I am the past. The world has turned; I can do no more," His eyes were glistening, and I almost reached out, "I'm about done, Con Rua. You are my last."

"Look," I said, "I'm grateful, but what do you want of me?"

"Pass it on,"

"You're asking me to take your place?" I said, "Is that what you're suggesting?'

"If not you, boy, then who? You have the gift, both in speaking and writing. You must pass this knowledge on, through your words and through your books. And you must do that freely, the same way it was given to you,"

"But the third circle," I protested, "I don't even know what it's about!"

"Before we are done, you will know."

I stared at him for a long moment, "Who am I supposed to help?"

"Start with that priest fella."

"But he's mad as a cut snake," I said.

"And you were sane when first we met?"

He turned, and I followed him to the door.

"When will I see you again?" I asked.

He didn't answer. He just stepped out into the night and disappeared.

CHAPTER 32

Commitments

I DIALED GISELLE'S number as soon as I got home, Tristan picked up on the third ring,

"Dad?"

"Yes, son, how did you know it was me?"

"We have a new phone; the number comes up on the screen."

"How are things at school?"

"It's getting better, my French is pretty good now. Will I have to learn Irish when we get to Inis Mór?"

"Irish is the first language here, Tristan, but most people have English too. The school's bilingual, Irish and English, and they have a couple of students here from France, so it won't be a problem."

"I'm not worried, Mum says I'm good at languages."

"That's great, Son. So, you'll be able to teach me Irish in a year or so."

"Conor?"

"Hi, darling. I was talking to Tristan about school. He's keen to learn Irish."

"How's the job going? Is Finbar working out?"

"Yes, he's great. They've moved into a cottage just up the road from the shed. It needs a few repairs, but they seem happy enough there."

"And you?"

"I miss you. Both of you. How are things over there?"

"Good, Dad seems to have improved a bit. The doctor said it's because Martine's here. He still asks for Mum in the mornings sometimes, but he's not getting angry like he was a few weeks ago. I just hope it lasts."

"You're still all right for Christmas?"

"Yes, of course, we're looking forward to being there. That won't change darling." She paused, "Conor, there was a woman on the news last night, Gabrielle Marcial. She's a famous French actor. She and her husband were on a sailing boat that sank near Inis Mór. She mentioned that it was a lifeboat from Inis Mór that saved them, and she said that one of the crew was Australian. Was that you?"

I hadn't wanted to mention it, afraid it might add to her concerns, "Yes, I was called out on the lifeboat that night."

"God almighty, Conor! What were you doing out in a gale on a lifeboat?"

"Giselle, the regular crew were over in Galway. They were desperate for volunteers. We were the only hope they had!"

"But you have a wife and child to consider! What were you thinking?"

"Darling! There was a young boy on the yacht, the same age as Tristan! I had no choice. If it were Tristan out there, would you want me to leave him to drown?"

There was a long silence.

"No, of course not, but you should have told me. You're so secretive! It's what you don't tell me that frightens me, Conor. I knew it was you on that lifeboat. I just knew. And she said your engines failed."

"They did, but not for long. Fitz went over the side and rescued the boy, and the skipper got the engines going quickly."

"Fitz saved the boy?"

"Yes, didn't she mention that?"

"She may have, I only caught half of the interview. Her husband's still in hospital with a concussion. He's an Irishman, from Galway, that's where they were heading when they lost their mast."

"I didn't know that. He was still unconscious when they choppered him out. How is he now?"

"She said he's concussed but recovering well. Are you okay?"

"I'm fine, a hundred percent, darling, don't worry."

"Of course, I worry! You're my husband. You've got to be more careful; you have a family to consider."

"Giselle, it was a once in a lifetime thing, it won't happen again."

"You'd refuse next time?"

"I hope not."

"Be careful, Conor, for our sake, be careful."

"Say hi to Martine," I told her.

CHAPTER 33

Anam Cara

WEDNESDAY WAS A clear, cold morning, frost heavy on the windowsill, my breath visible in the air. I pulled a blanket around my shoulders and went below. The ashes from the previous evening lay cold and grey in the grate. I began from the beginning. Paper, kindling, and a few small logs. Shivering on my knees, like a supplicant before an altar. The whispers of the kindling catching alight. The early, hesitant flames. The flickering light, then the smoke, ascending like a prayer to the heavens. I stayed there for some time, mesmerized by this ancient ritual, then rose and went out to the kitchen.

I brewed coffee, made toast, scrambled some eggs, then carried it all back into the living room, warming my feet as the fire crackled to life.

As soon as breakfast was done, I grabbed my bicycle and rode down to Cill Rónáin, an icy wind cutting at my eyes as I pushed hard on the pedals. As I rounded the final bend, I was surprised to see smoke rising from the shed, and when I eased through the wicket door, I found Fitz sitting in my armchair making notes.

"We can start in on the hull today," he looked up, "She's eighty years old if she's a day. Those broken planks have been drying out for years, so they'll be tight. We'll need a nail puller and a crowbar. But take it easy, we don't want her ribs damaged."

"I'll start on that," I said, "Some of the original decking has to be replaced too."

"Rot?"

"No, just wear. And there's some impact damage above where the hull was stove in."

Dierdre arrived at midday carrying a basket of food, and the three of us sat around the fire eating.

"Cillian's above with a lump of wood he found on the beach." She was smiling, "I left him there staring at it, he's waiting to see what it is,"

"How do you mean?" I asked.

"Well, when a nice piece like that comes to him, he'll study it for hours, sometimes days, before he'll touch it. He has a belief that the image is already in there, like a spirit, you know, and he must wait till it speaks to him."

"Where did he get a belief like that from?" I asked.

"No idea," she was shaking her head, "He's been working with wood since the age of seven. Fitz needed firewood onetime years ago, remember?" she looked across at Fitz, "There were planks that needed steaming, so we had a man deliver a load of rough wood for burning; mostly roots of old trees and the like. Well, Cillian pulled a big root out from the pile and set it up in the shed at home. It sat there for a week or more. Cillian was in there morning and night, staring at it. We thought it odd but didn't interfere. Well, he came in one evening after school and said to me, 'I know what it is, Ma, I know what's inside.'" She shook her head, "I didn't know what to make of it at the time, but it seemed harmless enough, so we just let him be."

"I wasn't allowed to see it," Fitz smiled, "Every time he was finished for the day, he had it covered over."

"So, what was it?" I asked.

"It was a head," Dierdre said, "A man's head. The first time I laid eyes on it, I wondered was it some sort of trick he was playing, it was that well done. The eyes, the hair, the face, like one of those statues you'd see in a museum. He took a photo of it and showed it to his art teacher. The next thing the teacher's knocking on our door telling us we had a genius on our hands, and could he enter the carving into the arts festival in Galway that year," she shrugged, "So we agreed."

"It won first prize," Fitz came in, "They had him in the Galway newspaper. But the teacher kept pestering to do more, to the point where Dierdre had to go up to the school and tell him to stop. After that he stopped carving altogether for a year."

"But he's back carving now, isn't he?"

"Yes, but he's his own man. He carves what he wants to carve, nothing else."

"He's a strange lad," I said.

"What would you expect?" Dierdre said, "With a man the likes of Fitz for a father and a selkie for a mother."

"A selkie!"

"Will you look at him," Fitz burst out laughing, "Sure, half the island's convinced she's a selkie, and you're not far behind by the look of ye'!"

"I don't listen to rumors," I said.

"No, I'm sure you don't. But it seems like they have you wondering!"

I turned to Dierdre, "You said, *your kind*, that day in the kitchen. What did you mean?"

"Did I not tell you to ask Fitz?"

"Is there such a thing as a selkie, Fitz?"

"No," he was still grinning, "And you should know better than to ask."

"So, what's Dierdre then? She's very different."

"She's a Traveler for God's sake, a Gypsy. Look at her. Is that not obvious?"

"A Gypsy! You said you met her by the ocean at Dún Leary?"

"That's right," he turned to his wife, "Tell him yourself if you will, but don't feel you have to."

"Fitz saved my life," she moved across to him, an arm around his waist, "That's how we met. I tried to kill myself, threw myself in the sea. He saw me drowning and dived in and pulled me out."

✧ ✧ ✧

I LISTENED TO her story then, Fitz's arm around her, tears in the darker parts.

"Every living creature believes that beauty is a great gift," she was shaking her head, "But there's many who were given that same gift might not agree. I came into this world thirty-three years ago as a Traveler, a Tinker, as we were once called. I was brought up on the road. My father was a powerful man, loved by many. My mother, a Romani Gypsy, beautiful but arrogant and willful." She paused, "I only have vague memories of her. She disappeared when I was six; ran off with another man I'm told. Da never once mentioned her. I'd catch him sometimes at night, staring at a photograph of her in a red dress. But he never once spoke of her, and we never asked. Travelers are proud people. Kind and loyal when respected, fierce when not. My father traded horses, travelling from one fair to the next. It's a close-knit community and gossip can be fierce. My brother Rory was five years older than me; a good lad, though he could be wild with a drink in him. That's how we came to grief." She paused and turned to Fitz, tears in her eyes.

"That's enough now, macushla," he brushed a tear from her cheek, "You've said enough."

"No, I want him to know, somebody should know," she turned back, "I was seventeen, and had never known a man. Protected by a father who thought the sun shone out of me," she paused, remembering.

"We were just outside Galway that year, waiting on a horse fair to start. We'd found a quiet place, off the road a bit, and set up camp. The following day we were joined by some Gypsies over from France. Well, they seemed decent enough people, and things were fine for a day or two, but when they returned to camp on the third evening they'd been drinking. There was a young woman with them, Roseen, she would have been five or six years older than me at the time. She was wild, Con. Beautiful but wild. You could see it in her. Long dark hair, flashing black eyes, and a smile that would have shamed the devil himself. Well, Rory couldn't take his eyes off her." she shook her head, "She frightened me, Con, I trembled whenever she was near me. There was something about her, a power. And a power she knew full well she had. And that's what frightened me, for I knew in my heart I wanted the same," she hesitated, "Men had been pestering me since the age of twelve. Telling me how beautiful I was, whispering, flirting. But I had no idea at all at that age, and it only served to make me shy. But when I saw what that woman could do to a man, what she did to my own brother, I felt a thrill, God forgive me, for I wanted the same.

"My father had gone out earlier that day, leaving Rory in charge. And when Roseen and the others returned, we watched them from the caravan. They lit a bonfire in the clearing and began cooking. Then one of them, a tall, dark man, came over to our van and asked was Dad home. When we told him no, he asked would we join them for supper. Rory said no, and told him we'd already eaten, although we hadn't. Then we watched through the window. There was seven of them, five men, Roseen, and an older woman. A little later the music started up, two fiddlers and a bowran drum, and then they were dancing. Roseen was the center of attention, whirling around the campfire, spinning, and turning like a wild woman. Rory staring, mesmerized." She paused again, gathering her thoughts, "She came over then, knocking on our door.

"'Will you not join us?' she asked Rory, a big smile on her face.

"'I can't,' he told her, I have to look after my sister.'

"'She's welcome too. Wouldn't it be better than the two of ye' just staring out the window all night?'

"'I'll come over in a minute, so,' he relented, 'but she's too young.'

"'What age is she?'

"'Seventeen,' he said.

"'Now then,' she said, 'Sure wasn't I married myself at sixteen! Get her ready and bring her over!'

"'You're married?' he asked.

"'Not anymore!' She laughed, and then she was gone.

"'Can I come?' I asked.

"'No,' he'd pulled on a clean shirt and was brushing his hair, 'Dad would go mad if he found out!'

"'But he won't be back for hours,' I told him, 'He said so himself,'

"'No!' he said, 'You're too young, you know that.'

"Then he was gone, out the door, leaving me watching them through the window. Drinking, laughing, dancing with Roseen. Oh God…" She raised both hands to her face, pulling them back tight through her hair, as if trying to tear away the memories, "I was so angry. But then I made up my mind. I went into my father's room and put on my mother's red dress. It was low cut, and tight around the body. Then I brushed back my hair like Roseen's, stepped out the door, and went over to the fire."

Dierdre stopped, her face in her hands, Fitz looked at me, shaking his head.

"There's no need to go further, macushla. Conor's heard enough."

"No! I need to finish." She went silent for a while, staring at her hands, "The music stopped when they saw me, and all the men stared. 'Dierdre,' Roseen called out, 'A glass of wine for Cinderella!' That's how it began. Wine, men crowding around, telling me I was beautiful, dancing. At first, I was shy, but after a few drinks that changed. Rory dancing with Roseen, me with different men. My confidence rising with each drink. A tall man with his arms around me, kissing me, whispering things in my ear; oh, dear God…"

She was shaking her head.

"It happened so quickly. My father came out of nowhere. He hit the man so hard he knocked him out cold on the ground. Then someone hit Da and Rory joined in. Men screaming and cursing, a bottle smashing over Rory's head, my father swinging a length of wood, but then stopping suddenly, the wood falling to the ground, his hands clutching his stomach, blood spilling out between his fingers…"

She broke down completely then. Sobbing into her hands as Fitz held her in his arms.

"Enough my love, enough," there were tears in his eyes now, "There's no need. Stop! For God's sake, stop."

"No, I've carried this too long," she raised her head again, "I don't know how long I held on to my father, Con. People running around, cars racing away. I don't know who called the ambulance. They arrived shortly after, but my father was dead by then. They took us all to the hospital. Rory had stitches in his head. They treated me for shock." She paused, "The police told us that they'd be interviewing us the following day, but when I went to check on Rory the next morning, he was gone. I took a taxi back to the camp. There was police tape on the ground by the door, but no sign of Rory. Just a note on the table, saying that he knew I could never forgive him. I lost my father and my brother that same night. It was too much to bear. I caught a bus to Salthill, walked to the end of the jetty, and threw myself in," she smiled then, her eyes filled with tears, "Fitz was there, and went in after me. The rest you know." She raised her eyes to meet mine, "We all have our burdens in life, Conor. It's how we rise from them what counts."

✧ ✧ ✧

THE FITZ'S LEFT early in the evening but I stayed on, working on the fastenings. The old iron nails were almost impossible to get out, but as I went along, I devised a system where I chipped away enough of the timber to expose the top of the nail, then gripped the head with a nail puller, and levered them out.

By seven o'clock I'd removed more than half, then I stopped. Fitz had warned me not to remove them all as that could weaken the hull too much.

I cleaned up the shed, washed my face in the sink, and closed the door behind me. It was Wednesday night. The meeting was at eight.

CHAPTER 34

Father Aiden

WHEN I ARRIVED at the hall, Aiden was already there, sitting on the steps, staring at the ground.

"Aiden, you're early."

"Sure, I had nothing else to do. I sit around that old cottage all day with Father Kiely, and he's no craic at all."

"I thought you were up there by yourself?"

"God no, I wish I was. Kiely's on leave of absence, same as myself. He was there before me; thinks he owns the place."

"So, what's his problem, or shouldn't I ask?"

"Oh, it's no secret. He's ninety years old with dementia and sticky fingers."

"Meaning what?"

"He's a kleptomaniac. Can't help himself, the poor man. Brigid has him barred from her place. He's been arrested a dozen times or more by the Gardaí in Galway. They know him well. They told the bishop he'd be jailed next time. He's been over here since."

"And you don't get on?"

"You try getting on with a ninety-year-old kleptomaniac you have to introduce yourself to each morning. He steals from me every day of my life and then forgets where he hides the stuff. Sure, my left shoe was gone today, I found it in the oven."

"So how are you holding up?"

"I'll not lie to you, Conor, it's wearing thin. I don't see any point to my life at all."

"But you're sober, Aiden, that's the main thing. We all get tested when we stop drinking. Hang in there and keep coming back."

Other people were arriving, the meeting was about to start.

"We'll have coffee after, okay?" I told him, "We can talk then."

That didn't happen, halfway through the meeting he got up and walked out the door, head down, hands in his pockets. I watched him go, knowing how he felt. But you can't chase alcoholics. If they don't want sobriety, there's no way you can sell it to them.

CHAPTER 35

Steaming Planks

MYSELF AND FITZ worked together the next day. Stripping off the damaged planks, cutting and shaping new ones. Not talking much, content in our work.

"You can start in steaming those planks, Con. Two at a time if you would. As soon as you take the second one out, get the next two in."

We were eating sandwiches, by the fire. We'd spent the morning selecting out lengths of oak. Cutting them to size, offering them up to the hull, making minor adjustments, then offering them back up again to make sure they sat right. Fitz was a perfectionist, the slightest blemish or fault, he'd discard a plank and start in on the next.

We'd ended up removing nine rows of planking. More than I thought was needed. They ran from the full length of the boat. From her stem to her stern, only one join allowed in each row.

"With that sort of damage on an old boat like this, it's best to err on the safe side," he was driving four-inch bronze screws into the first plank. A twenty-one foot long, three inches wide, one and a quarter inch thick length of larch. "It will help keep those ribs secure until we can replace them."

Once he had the first few screws in, I went below and

topped up the fire to ensure an even steam throughout. It took us all afternoon to get the planks in place, but by six that evening we were done.

"That's the easy part," he was putting his tools away, "Tomorrow, we'll start in on her ribs."

"Any steaming involved?"

"No, it's all cutting, and shaping. It's a lost art, but if you've a mind to be a boatbuilder, I don't mind teaching you what I know."

"I'd appreciate that," I told him, "I enjoy the work, and I'm going to need some sort of skill to earn money."

"I was surprised Dierdre trusted you with her story," he looked across at me, "She's never spoke of it to another living soul since the day it happened."

"I won't be repeating it," I told him, "Not to anyone."

"No, it's not that. She trusts you. She believes we've come together for a reason, and I feel the same. We're thinking of staying on here, Con. On the island I mean. I'm easy here, and for the first time in my life I feel I might belong somewhere."

"They think the world of you here, Fitz," I said, "The poetry night broke the ice."

"Your turn next. Do you have that story ready for Christmas?"

"Not yet. It's about a man called Peter Kagan and his wife who was a selkie, but there's a chorus to it and I can neither sing nor play a guitar."

"Come over for dinner tonight and talk to Dierdre. I'm sure she'd be happy to help."

✧ ✧ ✧

A PAINT SPECKLED Cillian opened the door when I arrived that evening, a brush in one hand, a multicolored rag in the other, Dierdre behind him smiling.

"Come in out of the cold and give me that coat."

"The place looks great." I said, "Are you nearly done?"

"Cillian's finishing off his own room, then there's only the bathroom left, and a few bits and pieces outside. What do you think?"

"It's a big improvement. You're happy here?"

"We both love it here, on the island I mean, and Cillian does too. He's set himself up in the shed out the back and he couldn't be happier."

I followed her into the sitting room, "Fitz, said you were thinking of staying on the island?"

"We are, do you not see the difference in the man? I've never known him so happy. I'm just after talking to an agent in Galway. He's off to Spiddal in the morning to give us an idea of what our place is worth. They've been out there a dozen times in the past few years trying to buy the place. It's one of the few big blocks left out there."

"Con," Fitz appeared at the back door with an armful of logs, "I forgot to mention to Dierdre about that story of yours, you can explain it to her yourself now?"

"Tell me after dinner," Dierdre stood up, "Come out and help me with the plates, Fitz."

✧ ✧ ✧

I WATCHED AS they said grace, heads bowed. Envying them the simplicity of a belief that I had long since abandoned.

As soon as the meal was over, we settled into chairs by the fire, and after Fitz had passed around fruit cake and tea, he joined us.

"So, this story of yours, was it given to you?"

"Yes, I heard an old fisherman in Brittany tell it to a group of tourists in a pub in Brittany one evening. I spoke to him after, and he told me that a seanachaí by the name of Gordon Bok created the story."

"And you met him?"

"No, but I called and asked for his blessing to repeat the story, and he gave that to me."

"Go on then, tell it to us."

"I will, but first you need to know there's a song involved, like a chorus. It comes in several times, and it's critical to the depth of the story. That's where I was hoping that Dierdre might help me."

"Sing it to us, so," she stood, "I'll get my guitar."

"Okay, but I don't have much of a voice."

When she came back, she tuned the guitar as I recounted the first part of the story. When I came to the first chorus I sang,

"Kagan, Kagan, Kagan
Don't go out to sea
Storms do blow and snow do come
And oh but I do fear for thee…"

"Well, it's a selkie story right enough," Fitz looked over at his wife, "Are you sure you'll be right with that, macushla?"

"Why not? Finish it now, Con. Just let me know when to

come in."

We ran through the whole story. Dierdre perfectly on cue each time. Me starting to feel more confident.

It was midnight when I left. Fitz asleep in an armchair, Cillian already gone to bed.

CHAPTER 36

Born Again

THE WEEKS ROLLED by. We were working from dawn to dusk. *Anam Cara* had beautiful lines, and once all the obvious damage had been addressed, we recalked her hull, sanded her smooth, then treated her to her first coat of paint in years. I suggested green, but Fitz was adamant.

"No, there's only one color for a hooker, Con, black. Down below you can do whatever you will, but the hull must be black."

Patrick had asked for an update on the work. So, I took interior and exterior photographs of *Anam Cara*, got Cillian to draw up detailed plans for the whole project, then sent it all off to Gwen. A few days later we received the go ahead from Patrick. The new cockpit was smaller than the one I'd stripped out, and Fitz explained why.

"With the low freeboard hookers can take on water in a blow if you're not careful. That's about their only fault, although they can be hard on the helmsman at times," we were fitting the rudder, "See the rake on that rudder, it can cause drag in heavy weather, especially when you're coming about."

"That's why the cockpit's smaller?"

"Yes, Patrick's thinking of taking her over to France. A small, well-drained cockpit, can be a lifesaver in a gale."

"Like *Erin's*?"

"Exactly, your grandfather knew what he was about when he converted her to a cruising boat. Following seas have sunk many a hooker. That little cockpit probably saved your life."

Once the rudder was done, we moved inside. The hull was a bare shell, a mass of ribs and stringers. We'd pulled out the cabin sole as we were concerned about rot and replaced it with teak, so we now had a solid floor to stand on. Cillian joined us with his plans, explaining the specifications for the coachroof.

"Do you see here now," Cillian was explaining why the beams on the aft end of the cabin were heavier and thicker than the rest, "Once the cabin's done, the sliding hatch will be bolted to these cross beams, and they need to be man enough for the job." He looked up at his father, "In a heavy blow, that hatch needs to be capable of surviving a wave running the full length of the boat, you know what it's like out there."

"I do, and that's the right choice."

"And we don't need oak on the coach roof, Da, larch is lighter and just as good."

"We'll go with larch, so."

"Now, I've allowed for a little detail work inside the cabin. It's not needed, I know, but Dr. Finlayson's looking at her as a leisure craft, so we might as well pretty her up a bit while we're at it."

"You're right." Fitz nodded. "It costs the same amount of money to build an ugly boat as a beautiful one."

We releveled the cradle to match her waterline, then began framing up the boat's interior. *Anam Cara* was twelve feet in the beam, plenty of room for a full-size berth on both sides, with storage areas behind the backrests and underneath the bunks.

"We'll use larch for the frames too," Fitz handed me a list of measurements, "There's plenty of it there below and it's an easy wood to work with."

I was sorting out lengths of timber when my mobile rang.

"Giselle?"

"Are you by yourself?"

"Yes, are you okay?" there was silence, "Are you there, Giselle?"

"Conor, I'm overdue. I'm pregnant."

"Jesus!" It took me a moment to get myself together, "That's fantastic! You must come over here now, darling. Don't argue, please. The cottage is free now. Fitz found another place."

"Are you sure you can look after us?" there was a falter in her voice, "I need to…"

I cut her off, "Giselle, we have our own house here and I have a good job. What more do we need?"

"Tell me you love me. Say it," she was in tears.

"Darling, have you forgotten the days we had in Brittany? Of course I love you, I always have. You're the reason I live. You're my waking thought and my final prayer each night. I don't know what else I can say to convince you…"

I waited, not even knowing if she was still listening.

"I'm frightened," she whispered.

"I know, but you'll come."

"Yes."

"When?"

"Martine's good with Dad. I trust her. We can be there before Christmas."

"Okay, that will give me time to fix up Tristan's bedroom and get some warmer things over from Galway," I paused, "You'll be happy here, darling, I know you will."

"Did you make enquiries about a school?"

"Yes, there's a good school here, Coláiste Naomh Éinne. They showed me around. It's a great little place. There are only a few weeks left till the end of term, so he can't start until January. Some of the classes are in Irish, but everyone speaks English too, so he'll be fine."

CHAPTER 37

Patrick

THE PHONE RANG at two am that night. I almost fell out of bed, struggling to reach it.

"Hello?"

"Conor, were you sleeping? What time is it over there? I should have checked."

"Patrick?"

"Yes, should I call back another time?"

"No, it's fine," I sat up, "What is it?"

"How's the boat coming along?"

"We're well ahead of schedule," I told him, "And she's looking good."

"Those photographs you sent over; I showed them to a friend of mine. He's the Commodore of a Yacht Club here in Boston. He's a nice guy; filthy rich, but a nice guy. Look, he wants to take a look at *Anam Cara*, and Fitz's boat too, if that's okay."

"Fitz's boat is not for sale, Patrick."

"Everything's for sale, Conor, if the price is right."

"Don't count on it." I told him, "But there's no harm looking. I'll check with Fitz, but it shouldn't be a problem. You know where the boat is."

"Any idea when we can get *Anam Cara* back in the water?"

"I'd say within six weeks. The cabin's well under way, and the cockpit too. There's only a few weeks of structural work left. After that it's just the paint, mast, deck fittings, and rigging. When will you be here?"

"We'll be in Dublin in three days, Galway a day or two after."

"And your mate wants a hooker?"

"Yes, his heart's set on it. Shamus O'Callahan's his name. Third generation Irish. His grandfather was a Connemara fisherman. He's stone mad for a hooker the same as mine. He has a few modifications in mind, wants to sail the boat back to the States. Are the two of you up for building a boat like that?"

"Patrick, Fitz is a master boatbuilder. He's been building hookers for years."

"I'll bring him over, so. And be aware, he won't want anything done on the cheap."

"It definitely won't be cheap, Patrick."

"Go back to sleep, Conor, I'll be there in a few days."

✧ ✧ ✧

THEY ARRIVED ON the late ferry five days later; standing out like cats at a canary show in their New York style suits and ties.

I shook hands with Patrick, "You stayed in Galway last night?"

"Yes. We had a look at Fitz's boat on the way through." He turned, "This is the man I told you about, Conor, Shamus O'Callahan."

"Conor," he was a big man, with a bone crushing handshake and a white tombstone teeth smile. "A pleasure to meet you."

"You too, Shamus. How long are you here for?"

"Well, it's all a bit rushed." Patrick said, "I have to be back in Boston by Thursday, but Shamus may stay on for a day or two longer."

"That's right," Shamus was looking around, "This is my first time in the old country and I don't want to spoil things by rushing."

"You're from Boston?"

"Yes, sir, Boston, Massachusetts, the capital of Ireland." He turned, "Lead the way, Patrick, I'm keen to get a look at this boat of yours."

"She's over in the shed," I told him, "Come on."

✧ ✧ ✧

FITZ WAS CUTTING timber for the mast as we walked in, crouched over the bench, his beard checkered with sawdust, and after brief introductions, he went back to work as I showed Patrick over *Anam Cara*.

"I just wish to God my father could have seen her like this before he passed." He was obviously delighted, "You've done a great job, the two of ye."

"She's sound now, Patrick." I told him, "All her fastenings have been replaced, and there's not a trace of rot in her anywhere. She'll be right for another eighty years by the time we finish with her."

"She's a beautiful boat," Shamus was examining every nook and cranny, "But forgive me Patrick, not as beautiful as

Dierdre." He turned to me, "Can we talk to Fitz about his boat?"

"She's not for sale," I told him.

"Let Fitz decide that, Conor. Shamus has his heart set on that boat."

Fitz was tidying up for the night when we got back down. Sweeping off the bench saw, putting away tools.

"Do you have time for tea, Fitz?" I asked, "Patrick wants a word."

"I'll make it," he said, "You pull up a couple of chairs."

"You've done a fine job on my boat, Fitz, I'm indebted to you."

"It's what we do here, Patrick, Conor and myself."

"We had a look at your own boat on the way through." Shamus was sitting forward in his chair, studying Fitz. "And I'll be honest with you, I'd love to own that boat."

"She's not for sale."

"You haven't heard an offer yet, Fitz, hear me out."

"No need, Shamus, like I said, she's not for sale."

"If she was for sale," Patrick came in, "What would you say she'd be worth?"

Fitz paused, looked down at the ground for a long moment, and when he looked back up, there was a spark in his eye.

"Not everything in this world's for sale, Patrick. I built that boat for three people. My wife, my son, and myself, in that order. The three of us have worked on *Dierdre* for the past twelve months. There's blood, sweat, and tears in that boat, and all of it ours. For the last time now, she's not for sale."

"Fitz..." Shamus began again, but I cut him off.

"She's not for sale, Shamus. I know Fitz. She's not for sale."

Fitz stood abruptly. "I have to be home, Conor. Goodnight all." And he was gone.

"Did I say something?" Shamus looked startled.

"He's easily upset," Patrick smiled, "He chased myself and Gwen off when we came out here last year."

"What I was about to say was, if she's not for sale, could you guys build me one the same? Exactly the same, I mean?"

"Why not?" I told him, "That's what we do here."

✧   ✧   ✧

THEY BOTH STAYED for three days. Shamus was in the shed every day, taking photographs and measurements, asking questions. Patrick up at the hotel working the telephones.

"Do you know of any hookers that were sailed from here to America?" Shamus asked one day.

"Yes, there's been a few sailed over there and back," I told him.

"Would you recommend any modifications for a trip like that?"

"For an ocean-going hooker I'd keep the cockpit small," I told him, "Same as my own boat. I wouldn't touch her lines; hookers are stable and fast on most points of the wind."

"So, why don't we get some ideas down on paper, draw up a set of plans?"

"We can do that. Cillian's the man for the job. He drew up the plans for his father's boat."

By the time they left there was a signed contract that Patrick had drawn up. Arrangements in place so that Gwen would take care of finances and any problems that might arise. A better relationship between Fitz and Shamus. And myself and Fitz back to finalizing the work on *Anam Cara*.

CHAPTER 38

Tristan and Giselle

My wife and son arrived on Inis Mór the following month, just two days before Christmas. The ferry emerging from a heavy mist like a ghost ship from a dream. Tristan was first to appear on the gangplank, Giselle close behind; I met them halfway down.

"Welcome to Inis Mór," I kissed my wife, then continued on down to where Mary and Lorcan were waiting.

"Thank God you're here safe," Mary had her arms around Giselle, "We were afraid they'd cancel with the fog."

"You go on ahead," Fitz had a suitcase in either hand, "Get them out of the cold. Cillian's gone up for Tessie. I'll have the bags sorted in no time."

As we walked back along the quayside, Tristan noticed the boatshed, "Is that where the boats are, Dad?"

"Yes, but we'll have breakfast first. We'll come back down later; okay?"

"Can I have a look now?"

"Is that okay?" Giselle, eyebrows raised, "He's talked of nothing else since we left home."

"Why not?" Dierdre asked, "You go on ahead Mary, we won't be long,"

"I have breakfast there now when you're ready."

"It will only take a minute or two at most," Dierdre turned, "Come on, Tristan, we'll take a quick look."

As we entered the shed Fitz joined us.

"Why all the chairs?" Giselle was looking around.

"There's a party to be held here Christmas Eve." Dierdre told her, "Poetry and storytelling. My husband's the poet, your man's the seanachaí."

"She's huge, Dad!" Tristan was looking down from *Anam Cara's* cockpit, "We could sail back to Australia in her!"

"It's not our boat Son, we're just repairing her." I climbed the ladder, he was down below, inspecting the cabin, "Did you do all this, Dad?"

"Myself and Fitz," I told him, "Fitz is the boatbuilder, I'm the apprentice."

"What's that?"

"An apprentice is someone who learns a trade from a master craftsman, Son, and Fitz is all of that."

Dierdre's voice came floating up, "Come on now, Conor. Mary's waiting above."

✧ ✧ ✧

BOSON GREETED US as we approached the cottage, wriggling and twisting, excited to be meeting new family members. Lorcan opening the front door as we came up the path.

"Come in, all of ye." He had an egg flip in one hand. "Do you know how to cook, Tristan?"

"Not really."

"Well, you can help me with the toast then, make sure I don't burn it."

Mary was stepping down off a chair as we entered, decorations in one hand, scissors in the other, a Christmas tree lying in the hallway.

"Everything's ready, we can start serving right away. Give me a hand with the plates, if you would Dierdre. There's bacon and black pudding on the tray, Loran's putting the eggs on now."

We ate then, Lorcan fussing about, sliding eggs from the frying pan straight onto our plates. Mary offering toast, Giselle trying to help, Fitz getting stern with her.

"You sit down there now and do as you're told. You're the guest of honour here today and you're not to lift a hand."

"You can give me a hand with the Christmas tree after breakfast, if you would, Giselle." Mary had a hand on her shoulder, "I wanted a real one this year. Those plastic ones are never the same."

I was getting up to clear the dishes when Giselle touched my arm.

"Tristan wants to go back to the boatshed with you."

"Maybe later," I said, "We need to take everything up to our place and get settled in."

"Conor, he wants to go there with you. Just the two of you."

"Oh, I didn't realise. Yes, of course we can."

"Go off now then, I'll take care of the dishes."

✧ ✧ ✧

WE WALKED DOWN to the quayside together. The fog had lifted, a pale sun seeping through low hanging clouds. The breeze cool enough to keep your hands in your pockets. Boson striding on ahead.

The fire was burning low as we arrived, Tristan asked could he build it up, and I watched as he collected offcuts of timber and a few logs from the corner pile.

"You'll need to rake out the ashes, too," I told him, "That allows a draught to get in underneath."

"I know, Dad. I've done it before in Granddad's house."

"Do you drink tea?"

"No thanks, I'm fine."

He finished with the fire and sat down in my armchair.

"So, what do you think of Inis Mór?" I asked.

"Is Lorcan my grandfather?"

"Not really," I told him, "But he's like a grandfather, and Mary too."

"So, she'll be my grandmother?"

"Yes, they're both family."

"Can I help you build the boat?"

"Sure you can. But you'll have to start at the bottom, same as I did. You know, sweeping up the shed, looking after the tools. It's all important work."

"Do you think I'll be a boatbuilder too?"

"I don't know, Son. That will depend a lot on you. I won't push you one way or the other. Remember what we talked about in Brittany? About finding out what your gifts are?"

"Mum says I'm good at languages."

"That's a great gift." I told him, "You'd have others too."

"Do you know what they are?"

"Not yet, although I have noticed some things about you."

"Like what?"

"Well, you ask a lot of questions, that tells me that you have an inquisitive mind. You're good with animals, I noticed that on your grandfather's farm."

"That's a gift?"

"Yes, it's a part of who you are, and it's a positive thing."

"Anything else?"

"You're careful and considerate, those are gifts. And you're protective of your mother."

"How do you mean protective?"

"Well, I noticed you seemed a bit wary of me when I was over in Brittany. That's not a criticism, Son. I think you were concerned for your mother."

And suddenly he was in tears, wiping his face with the arm of his jacket.

"You hurt her, Dad. You just disappeared. Mums never said anything bad about you, but I don't want you to hurt us again."

My heart almost stopped. I rose and went across to him.

"Son, I was sick in Australia, but that's not a good excuse. I drank too much, way too much." I could hardly get the words out, "It was wrong, Son, very wrong, and I'm sorry. You deserved better than that, both of you."

He had his arms around my neck, and I could feel his tears on my cheek.

"Don't Leave us, Dad. Promise you won't leave us again." He was sobbing.

"Tristan, I swear to God, I will never leave you again. It's going to take a while for you to believe me. I know that. But I will never leave you again, Son, no matter what."

He held on to me for a long time, and when we finally let

go he looked directly at me.

"I believe you now, Dad. So does Mum. She told me that, before we left Grandad's place."

We walked back together then. The barrier between us, dispelled by tears. Boson walking alongside Tristan now, as if to protect him from harm.

CHAPTER 39

The Fili of Inis Mór

I WOKE EARLY Christmas Eve morning to an eerie silence and raising up on an elbow I understood why. The snow had continued falling throughout the night, and there was six inches or more resting on the windowsill. I eased out of bed quietly and peered through the glass at a landscape like none I had ever seen before. A dark blue ocean in the background. Snow drifting down sideways over rocks and fields. The island transformed into a magical fairyland by a clean, white blanket. Removing every stain, purifying, and forgiving, like a blessing from above.

I smoothed the doona around Giselle's face, pulled on a dressing gown and closed the door quietly behind me. Then I eased open Tristan's door, he was fast asleep, so I went below. There was still life in the embers. I arranged kindling, placed a few small logs on top, then opened the back door and stepped outside. It was surreal, utterly beautiful. And in that moment, I was overwhelmed by a sense of gratitude. I walked out into the snow barefoot and knelt, and raising my hands to the heavens, I thanked a Power whose name I did not know, for everything it had done for myself and for my family. I read somewhere once that grace is an unearned gift from God, and for the first time in my life, I understood the full meaning of those words.

How long I was there, I do not know, but at some point I felt a touch on my shoulder and Giselle was kneeling beside me.

We didn't speak. An arm around each other. The silence an unspoken prayer, pure and unadorned.

✧ ✧ ✧

WE SPENT THE morning wrapping gifts. Giselle and Tristan had brought presents from Brittany, and I had the gifts I'd bought in Galway.

"I have to be down at the boatshed by midday," I told Giselle, "I want to check the lighting."

"You're nervous?"

"Yes. Last time I blew it. Everyone will be there tonight."

"Think of this morning," she kissed my cheek, "And just be yourself."

Tristan fed Tessie at midday, then we strapped her into the trap, loaded up all the parcels, and trotted down to the boatshed. The Fitzgerald's were already there, making last-minute changes. Fitz had welded up a new steel brazier and was loading it up with timber as we arrived.

"That will make the difference," he was enjoying it all, "Cillian's never had a real Christmas, God forgive me, but we'll make up for it this year."

"How many people are coming?" I asked Dierdre, "Do we know?"

"There'll be a hundred or more. There's the Irish dancing on over in the big hall, so that will thin the crowd a bit, but don't worry, it'll be a full house."

I found no comfort in her words. That was exactly what

was worrying me.

✧ ✧ ✧

We opened the doors at four thirty and the early birds began filing in. Standing around the brazier, dressed up as if for church. The women helping with the food, the men talking and laughing among themselves. The hotel was fully booked for the Christmas, and a group of American tourists had arrived at the boatshed early and had taken up chairs close to the front. That hadn't helped my nerves much either. The shed filled quickly, and at six o'clock Lorcan moved to the center of the room and held up a hand.

"Ladies and gentlemen, and all the rest of you too," a ripple of laughter, "Before we begin, there's been a few changes to the evening. As most know these nights are usually conducted in the Irish language, tonight however, out of respect for our American guests, much of the poetry and song will be spoken in English, God forgive us," there was more laughter, "Now, to begin, we have with us tonight one of Ireland's greatest poets, Finbar Fitzgerald, and Finbar will be giving us a few of his poems for half an hour or so. Then we'll have a break for tea and coffee. We also have with us, Conor O'Rourke, the son of the late Con Rua O'Rourke, the Seanachaí of Inis Mór, and once the break is over, Conor will be telling us a story. Following that, you can forget about the tea and coffee and have a drop of the hard stuff, if you're so inclined! But, to begin the evening, please welcome Finbar's wife, Dierdre Fitzgerald."

I lowered the lights as Dierdre entered the circle. She

crossed to the chair, guitar in hand, then turned.

"This is a special night, a holy night," she looked around, "So I will sing for you one of the greatest of all the Christmas carols, Silent Night."

There was a hush as took her seat and began, her fingers strumming gently, her head thrown back, her body swaying, her voice loud and clear,

> *"Silent night, holy night*
> *All is calm, all is bright,*
> *Round young mother*
> *virgin and child*
> *Holy infant so tender and mild*
> *Sleep in heavenly peace*
> *Sleep in heavenly peace."*

She paused, "It's everyone's Christmas, so, if you will, join in the chorus…" and they did. She sang each verse; the whole shed sang the chorus. As she drew it to a close there was applause and demands for more, but Dierdre held up a hand.

"Thank you, but this night is for poetry and storytelling…" she swept a hand around behind her, "Now, please welcome my husband, Finbar Fitzgerald."

I'd dimmed the lights as there were so many strangers there, but as he arrived by Dierdre's side, he waved across at me.

"Raise the lights, Conor, let's not be shy tonight."

Dierdre kissed him, and as she left the circle, Fitz took his place in the captain's chair.

"Tonight is different," he began, "Most of my poems are in

Irish. But for tonight, considering our American friends, I sat with Conor O'Rourke today, and together we dreamed up a few words about Inis Mór." He settled back in the chair, "And this first poem we called, 'A Dream of Inis Mór.'"

He settled back in his chair, the seaman's cap tilted at an angle, his black unruly hair framing a face at peace with itself and the world…

"I have known the longing
Known that I was lost
I knew it as a child
Before the open door

I knew it as a stranger
Upon the foreign shore
That feeling left me only
When the name came—Inis Mór

It brought with it a yearning
A calling from my soul
A place I'd ever feared
I'd been so long alone

It carried with it sorrow
The opening of some door
When I heard the name I knew
An angel stood on Inis Mór

I lost my way long years ago
I faltered and I strayed

RETURN TO INIS MÓR

I turned away from those I loved
These choices I have made

But now at night I wonder
Could I return once more
Could I return to what I was
By the cliffs at Inis Mór

I swore an oath long years ago
That I would follow soul
I've stumbled and betrayed myself
More than I have told

Now I stand on foreign beaches
And know I am no more
And weep as night dark angels
Call the name of Inis Mór

Sometimes there is no logic
As to meaning or to cause
Sometimes the heart must rule the head
Unless we die as slaves

Sometimes at night I lay there
Called by spirit to that shore
And know an Angel's waiting
By the cliffs at Inis Mór

Night waves turning seeking
A half open dark door

Whispered lost memories
From that hard broken shore

Black waves rolling over me
Dark down from the deep
Where lies my purpose
Where will I sleep
Where will I sleep
Where will I sleep"

There was a smattering of applause as Fitz brought the poem to an end, and a few questions.

"Thank you Finbar," she was an American woman, around fifty or so, slim, elegant, "That was lovely. Could I ask where the inspiration comes from, the words I mean?"

"I'd tell you if I knew," he smiled his crooked smile, "Myself and Con Rua got together when we heard you were coming. We sat around the fire for a few hours and the words just came. It works that way at times. It's almost like getting out of the way of something that's already in you. Conor's part poet and part seanachaí, so it flowed easy between the two of us."

"Do you have any other poems about the island," a guy wearing a bright red ski jacket rose from his chair, "Like something I can take back to New England. I teach English Lit at home," he added.

"There is another one we have. It's about how this island draws people. Like Dierdre and myself. It happened to Conor too. It's as if you know the place somehow and are being called back, called on to return. Hard to explain, but here it is…"

RETURN TO INIS MÓR

He settled into the chair…

"I knew this island long before I ever came
Some hidden memory held in kind
Images of needing to forsake
An unused life in place

A turning from and a turning to
A knowing of the heart
A feeling to return unto that lonely dark
A memory of birth and death
And yet a singing lark

A star dark, whispered presence
What hails to Inis Mór
A wizened hand across a plank
A ticket to that shore

Standing still on winter's ferry
Snowflakes and frozen eyes
An age-old questing
For that rocky shore before my eyes

Held fast mid rock strewn waters
Knowing I had been
Ten thousand times upon this shore
In misted dreams

Far from the gilded city
Away from once called home

A coursing, rolling, dipping, sailing
Towards the Soul's intoned

An unspoken, restless yearning
From a mind deranged by sun
A burnt-out lost remembering
From where it all began

A passage back in time
To where the pieces wait
A coming home to birthing
Carried by some deeper place

Returning fragments
From a shadowed, empty past
Recognition of a land
My soul held fast

A sensing, coursing, homing feeling
I'd never touched before
A heartfelt sense of loss and pain
The opening of some soul swung door

To the rain swept rocky wind wet cliffs
and fields of Inis Mór
To a meeting of an image held in place

A keening, keeling, wailing song
A grief that I was back
A heartfelt sense of age

without a track

No words to speak the loss
The land from which she bore
The jagged rocks
And sea scream birds that soar

Welcoming me, as they had before
Forgiving me my absence
As they waited by the shore
Returning to the rock and stone of Inis Mór……"

Everyone applauded, people crowding around Fitz at the break, some wanting autographs, others asking where they could buy his books.

CHAPTER 40

Peter Kagan and the Wind

I SAT WITH Tristan and Giselle during the break, drinking coffee, trying to relax.

"Why don't you tell them the story you told me, Dad?" Tristan had sensed I was uptight, "Mum tried to tell it me again, but yours was better."

"I have another one," I told him, "And Dierdre's going to sing the chorus for me,"

"It's a song?"

"No, it's a story. You'll understand better when you hear it."

Lorcan was ringing a small brass bell, people returning to their seats.

"Tell the story to me, Conor," Giselle was holding my hand, "I'll be in one of the front seats. Just look at me and tell me the story."

"I will," I told her, "I will."

Lorcan was wrapping up the introduction, "…so, please welcome Conor O'Rourke."

I was conscious of my awkwardness as I approached the chair, cursing myself for being so nervous. I couldn't see Giselle anywhere, but as I looked around, I caught a glimpse of a face outside one of the windows. It looked like the old man. I waved without thinking and a few of the people in the crowd waved back. Then, as I turned and took my seat, Dierdre joined me, carrying her guitar.

"You have this now, Con," she whispered, "just relax and tell the story."

I settled into the chair, my heart thumping.

"My name's Conor O'Rourke," I told them, "And there are people here tonight who knew my father. People who knew him better than I ever did. He was killed in a car crash in Dublin when I was eight years of age. I was in the car with him. After that my mother took me to Australia with her, wanting a fresh start." As I continued, I realized that I was starting to relax, "She remarried over there, married an Englishman. And I went from being Conor O'Rourke to John Carlyle. There's no one to blame for that, but I know now that it took the foundation out from underneath me, and over the years I forgot everything I knew about Ireland, and" I paused, "I guess I lost track of who I was in the process." I took a deep breath, "But before I go on, I need to tell you something. The truth is, my life fell apart in Australia, you know, drinking, drugs, and so on. And at my lowest ebb, I began hearing voices in my mind urging me to return to Inis Mór. Well, I followed those voices and that's why I'm here with you tonight."

I stopped speaking, unsure of where I was headed. The old man had told me that at times like this, I should ask for help.

"Ask who?" I asked.

"The Life Force, boy, allow the Force to flow through you,"

I looked across at the window, there was no one there, *please help me and guide me*, I mumbled, *please help me and guide me...* then I began...

"The story I'm about to tell you was first told by a man by the name of Gordon Bok. A famous seanachaí, singer, and songwriter, from Camden, a seaside village on the coast of Maine. It's a tale of a man by the name of Peter Kagan, and the selkie, who was his wife."

As I continued, Dierdre began strumming her guitar.

"Now stories of the selkies have been told for hundreds of years. Here on Inis Mór, up in the Hebrides, off the coast of Scotland, in the fishing villages of Donegall and West Kerry, and over in America, around Boston. For it is believed that in every village there is at least one family descended from the seal people. Now there are some among you that might know the story I'm about to tell, for it has been told for over fifty years and is one of the most famous of all the selkie legends. And I pass it on to you now, with Gordon's blessings…"

I paused, asked for guidance, then began…

"Peter Kagan was a lonely man in the summer of his years. But then one day he got tired of being lonely, and he went away off to the east. And when he came back again, he had a wife with him. She was strange you know, but she was kind, and people liked her. And she was good for Kagan, she kept him company. And winter come to summer, and they were happy.

"Kagan had a dory then, with a lugsail on her mast. He'd go offshore for three, four days, setting for the fish. And oh, his wife was sad then. She never liked to see him go. And if she knew that bad weather was coming, she'd go down to the water's edge, and she'd call to him."

Dierdre came in then, strumming louder, her voice ethereal, the islanders silent and still,

> *"Kagan, Kagan, Kagan*
> *Bring the dory home*
> *The wind and sea do follow thee*
> *And all the ledges calling thee."*

"And he said he could hear her singing twenty miles to sea," I continued, "And when he heard her, he'd come home, if he had fish or none. She was a seal, you know. Everyone knew that, even Kagan, he knew that. But nobody would say it to him."

I paused for a moment, looking around, and as I did, I realized that people were staring, not at me, but at Dierdre.

"Then, one day, in that year's autumn, Kagan said to his wife, 'I've got to go now. Go offshore and get some fish.'

"But she said, 'No! Don't go!' She starts crying. 'Please don't go. The wind is coming and the snow.'"

Dierdre came in again, her voice soft but strong,

> *"Kagan, Kagan, Kagan*
> *Don't go out to sea*
> *The stormy wind and snow do come*
> *And, oh, but I do fear for thee."*

"But Kagan's not afraid of snow," I continued, "It's early in the year, so he puts his oars in, and he goes out to sea. Kagan sails out on the middle ground. The Wind is west all day and going down, and the fish are coming to him. Kagan reads the writing on the water and the sky. He sees the haze up very high above the clouds and he says, 'That's all right for autumn, only a change of wind. I'm not afraid of wind.'

"But Kagan reads it wrong this time. For the Wind goes away, but then comes back again, southeast. The fog comes 'round him, and Kagan says, 'I'd better go now. Find that gong buoy off the sunken ledges, then I'll know the best way home.' He puts the sail up and bears away to the nor'ard for the gong. But, oh, the Wind is watching.'

I paused, some of the children had left their parents and were sitting on the sawdust floor in front of me.

"The Wind backs around to the east'ard then and gets stronger. They sail for a long time, and the sail is pulling very hard. Finally, the Wind is so strong, the sail tears out. Kagan takes it in, and the dory goes a-drifting. But then he hears the gong buoy. It isn't very far away.

Kagan, Kagan, Kagan
Bring the dory home
The wind and sea do follow thee
And all the ledges calling thee.

"But the dory goes a-drifting, and by and by the gong buoy goes away. Kagan says, 'Okay.' He puts the oars in and starts to row back up for the gong. But, oh, the Wind is watching. The Wind backs around Northeast, and makes the seas confused. The Wind says, Listen! I have something to tell you.'

"Kagan, rowing, 'I don't want to hear it.'

"The Wind humps up now, makes the sea short, making it hard for him to row. Finally, the seas are so steep, Kagan knows he isn't getting anywhere. He takes the oars in, and again, the dory goes a-drifting.

"Then Kagan says, 'Okay. Now I've got something to show

you.'

"He takes a slip of wood to make a needle and waxes up a hand line for a thread. He sews the sail up smaller, sews a reef in it.

"The Wind says, 'What're you doing?'

"Kagan says, 'You, keep watching.'

"Kagan puts the sail up now and again he bears away to the Nor'ard for the gong.

"But, oh, the Wind is watching. The Wind backs, north-nor-east, and Kagan can't hold his course now. Kagan says, 'Okay, then.' And he brings the boat about. Now he's steering east.

"The Wind says, 'You're heading out to sea.'

"Kagan says, 'I'm not afraid of water, I'll come about by-and-by when I can fetch that gong.'

"The Wind says, 'I'll veer on you; I'll go east again.'

"Kagan says, 'You go ahead, I can hold my course then.'

"The Wind says, 'I'll be back.'

"Kagan says, 'You back too far and you'll have to clear, you know that. I can keep ahead of you.'

"The Wind says, 'You may be smarter but I'm stronger, you watch.'

"The Wind gets bigger then, and blows harder, and finally, there's too much wind.

"The Sail says, 'I can't do it!'

"Kagan says, 'I know that. Thank you.'

Kagan, Kagan, Kagan
Turn ye now to me
Turn thy back unto the Wind

And all the weary windy sea.

"He takes the sail in then, and the dory goes a-drifting. Then Kagan takes the sail off the yard, he folds it around him and tells the sail, 'Sail, keep me warm.'

"But the Wind says, 'The sail can't keep you warm.'

"The Wind snatches off north by east and tells Kagan, 'I'll freeze you.'

"Kagan says, 'I'm not afraid of cold!'

"But Kagan is afraid. He doesn't know what to do. And oh, the Wind is working now. The Wind brings ice and snow. The Wind blows long, and hard, and black.

"Kagan says, 'I'm dying. Sail, keep me warm!' The sail says, 'I can't. I'm sorry, but I can't.'

"Kagan dying, and the wind blows."

Dierdre's voice took on a more plaintive note,

"Kagan, Kagan, Kagan
Lay ye down to sleep
For I do come to comfort thee
All and thy dear body keep."

"Kagan lies down in the bottom of the boat and tries not to be afraid of the dying. And he dreamed of her then, his wife. He dreamed she was coming to him, and he heard a great calling, coming down the wind, and lifting himself up on an elbow, he saw her coming to him. Down the smoking sea she came, and over the rail of the dory she came, laughing, into his arms.

And all in the night and the storm they did lay, and the

Wind and the Sea went away. And in the morning, they found him there, asleep, with a sail wrapped around. And there was a seal, lying there with him, curled over him like a blanket, and the snow inches deep upon her back..."

✧   ✧   ✧

THE SILENCE WENT on for so long after I finished, I thought I'd blown it. But then the whole room stood and began clapping.

As I held my hand out to Dierdre, the clapping increased.

"Con Rua O'Rourke," she slipped an arm around me, "like father, like son.,"

People were crowding around, shaking hands, asking questions, some of the children touching Dierdre, as if to see if she was real.

As applause faded, Lorcan was back in the center of the room, "Ladies and gentlemen, it's Christmas Eve. There's plenty of food and drink to be had, so, let's clear away the chairs, and get down to business!"

CHAPTER 41

The Céilí

That was how the Céilí began. Men and women carrying baskets of food and drink. People arriving with fiddles, penny whistles and bowran drums. A man with uilleann pipes clearing a circle. Aiden organizing drinks for the musicians, a broad smile on his face, a spring in his step. I pulled him aside.

"Aiden," I whispered in his ear, "Leave the drinks to someone else, mate, you just pass the food around."

"You have no faith in me at all," he said, "do you?"

"None whatsoever," there was a whiff of alcohol about him, but I wasn't sure, "So I need you to prove me wrong."

"I'll do as you ask," he grinned, "But the thought of a drink never crossed my mind till you mentioned it."

"Keep it up mate," I told him, "I'm proud of you." I watched as he walked away, there was a definite wobble in his stride.

Moments later the fiddlers kicked off with a mad Irish reel, and within minutes the shed came alive. The music rising, men and women dancing, older people and children sitting by the walls clapping.

I went across to the fireplace. Dierdre was adding logs to the rising flames.

"Have you eaten?" I asked.

"Fitz is over there now getting us something."

"You did a great job, Dierdre," I told her, "Thank you."

"You were the star," she said, "I was just the chorus."

"It's the chorus that makes the story," I told her.

"We've had an offer on our place in Spiddal," she looked up, "Did Fitz tell you?"

"No, when was this?"

"The agent called last night. They've been chasing after that land for years. Sure, he had buyers waiting."

Giselle and Fitz joined us, carrying plates of food.

I dragged an old seaman's trunk across and set it up as a table.

"There's turkey there and ham, and fresh soda bread," Fitz was laying it all out, "And there's Christmas cake under the cloth."

"Would anyone like a drink?" It was Aiden, eyes glazed.

Giselle and Dierdre ordered wine, Fitz a glass of porter, I ordered mineral water.

"It's Christmas, Conor!" the priest had a Jack Nicholson style grin on his face, "Will you not have a drop of the good stuff?"

"Are you okay, Aiden?" I asked.

"Never better!"

"Leave him be, Con," Dierdre whispered.

"He's drunk," I told her.

"Maybe, but Christmas is not the best of times to be to be getting off the drink."

"Stick to the Guinness." I told him, "No spirits; okay?"

"You have my word," he gave me a military style salute before disappearing into the crowd. I turned back to Fitz.

"You've had an offer on your place?"

"Yes, they want to develop the land."

"Are you going to accept?"

"That depends. Look, I hadn't planned on discussing this tonight, but we might as well now that we've started," he looked around, "Come in a bit," We drew our chairs closer, huddling around the makeshift table like a group of conspirators, "We're thinking of putting in an offer on the cottage we're renting. It has more than an acre of land with it," he looked at me, "Room enough for a good-sized shed."

"For building boats, you mean?"

"Why not? We already have one order, and I know there's others interested."

"He frightens them," Dierdre was shaking her head, "We had a man come out to Spiddal wanting him to build a boat, but he chased him away."

"Ah, that eejit! Sure, I didn't want him sailing around in any boat that I built," he turned back, "Look, Con, I'm no good at the business side of things; that's the truth. And that's where yourself and Giselle might come in."

"What are you suggesting?"

"I thought we might be partners. It was Dierdre's idea, and she's right. We work well together."

"But you could do it yourself," I told him, "You and Cillian."

"No, Cillian's an artist, not a boatbuilder. He's been offered a scholarship in Dublin. But if your boy's so inclined, he could maybe join us later, when he's a bit older. What do you think?"

"What would a partnership look like?"

"Fifty-fifty. Equal partners, the four of us. We do the

American's boat first, then we'll have a better idea of what's needed. But fifty-fifty, I'd want it no other way."

I spotted the priest weaving through the crowd, a tray of drinks held shoulder high in one hand. But then he swerved suddenly and took a detour around the far side of *Anam Cara*.

"What did the other guy want," I asked Fitz, "The one you chased off?"

"He was looking to have a Bad Mór built, the same as my own boat."

How long ago was that?"

"Three months or so," Dierdre came in, "He's a Dublin man. I have his details."

"Maybe we can still get that job…" The priest hadn't reappeared, "Could you excuse me for a moment?"

He was sitting in a pile of sawdust behind *Anam Cara*, finishing off our drinks as I approached.

"You're a gentleman and a scholar, Conor," he went to stand but almost fell over, "And there's not many of us left."

"God, you're a mess," I said, "How many weeks' sobriety did you have up?"

"Six weeks and five days," he grinned, "A personal best!"

"We'll start again after Christmas." I told him, "Don't give up, okay?"

"No surrender!" He went to salute again but slumped over sideways into the sawdust. I put my hand on his shoulder.

"Stay there, Aiden," I told him, "You're okay, mate. Stay there and sleep it off."

He closed his eyes, and I stood watching him for a moment, knowing there was a good heart in him somewhere, praying he'd find it one day.

"That's you, right there on the floor, Con Rua."

I spun around. The old man was sitting on the bottom bar of the cradle, smoke rising from his pipe.

"Not anymore," I told him, "Thank God."

"You stay with him. Do you hear me? Stick with him. He has no purpose in life and he's carrying the burden of shame. Find something for him to do. Sweeping the floors, making tea, sanding the hull, anything. And make sure he gets to those meetings."

"I've been trying to help him for weeks; he just can't seem to stop drinking."

"No, but you're sober. You were on the edge of picking up a drink when you met him. You pass it on, and you stay sober. That's the lesson. Get back to your family now, they're waiting for you."

"Are you going to join us?"

"I've left something for you," he nodded, "It's the only copy."

"A book?"

"Do not waste it."

"Waste what?" The priest was up on one elbow, trying to rise from the sawdust. "Sure, I've never wasted a drink in my life."

I bent and pushed him back down gently. "You're okay," I told him, "Go back to sleep."

When I turned back, the old man had disappeared. I looked around; someone was singing, "Red Sails in the Sunset." I walked through the crowd to the makeshift bar. A woman was standing on the bench singing; Brigid serving drinks.

"Could I get a pint of porter, two glasses of wine, and a mineral water please, Brigid?"

"Ha! The same order as that preacher fella! Where is he now?"

"He's sleeping it off, behind *Anam Cara*."

"I'll get him a blanket so."

I poured the drinks myself and took them back. Mary and Lorcan had joined our group.

"We thought you'd left us," Giselle looked up, "Where were you?"

"I was talking to the priest," I told her, "He's mad drunk."

"Conor, that one boat for the American man would give you six month's work or more," Lorcan had a hold of my sleeve, "That would give you plenty of time to find the next job."

"I know," I told him, "But I have to talk it over with Giselle."

"You can use the shed here as long as it's standing. Although it's due to be pulled down before the end of next year."

The music was starting again, dancers back on the floor, people calling out requests.

"Give us the Siege of Ennis!" or, "How about the Walls of Limerick?"

As the music rose, new lines formed, eight people in each group, two lines of four, kicking up their heels. Others, taken by the music, dancing in pairs. Tim all smiles, careening around with a tall, black American woman. Tristan and Cillian dancing with two young girls, and then, to my astonishment, Brigid came twirling through the center of the dancers with Aiden; he was grinning like a lunatic, heels kicking up.

I threw caution to the wind then and took Giselle out on the floor. The rising notes of the fiddles, the wailing of the eullain pipes, and the throbbing of the bowran drums, dispelling any trace of shyness. My inhibitions flying out the window as the music stirred age old genes that had lain dormant for years.

The energy was fierce, the life force gone mad. The spirit of Inis Mór, the same spirit that countless invaders failed to quell, vibrant and alive on this magical little island.

✧ ✧ ✧

Around eleven the crowd began to thin. Couples with children, calling out Christmas greetings, kissing friends. Our group was back by the fireplace, Giselle sitting in my lap, Tristan asleep in the other armchair.

"It could turn into something big," Lorcan was ruminating. "The O'Rourke's built boats on this island for years. That's where all that timber came from. Your grandfather had a mind to build a Bad Mór for himself."

"You can discuss all of that over the holidays," Mary was looking at her watch, "Midnight Mass starts in forty minutes. We'll need to get up there now if we're to find a seat."

We walked up to the church together. Giselle holding on to one of my arms, Tristan the other; Mary and Lorcan ahead of us. The snow had stopped falling and Inis Mór looked like a painting. A thick, white blanket of snow covering the roofs of each cottage. Lights from their Christmas trees glittering in the windows. Thick frost topping the old stone walls like icing on a cake. The sky above crystal clear, stars standing out like sparks on a charcoal canvas. A curious black cat, placing one careful paw in front of the other, cautiously creeping towards home.

A choir was singing as we approached the church; a carol I had known since childhood: "Adeste Fideles, Come all ye Faithful;" and I felt a stab in my heart. The longer I stayed on this island, the more I realized how much I'd let slip from my life.

The heart holds all that is truly important. It holds it now and forever. We change, and change, and change again. But what is real and true remains within us. And I felt that deeply as we moved through the snow towards that ancient place. My parents had married in this church, my father's body had lain there prior to his burial. All my ancestors knew and respected this holy place. It did not matter what religion I was; nor whether I knew the prayers or hymns or not. I was approaching my Soul's intent, and I felt the reverberations throughout my body. I paused at the church doors, overcome by emotion, Giselle's face touching mine.

"You're home, Conor," she whispered, "You're home at last."

CHAPTER 42

Christmas Day

CHRISTMAS MORNING, I woke early, a dream, or perhaps an intuition, stirring me from sleep. I kissed Giselle's face gently, then eased out of bed. I pulled on jeans, jumper, leather jacket and boots, and walked down to the boatshed, the snow too deep for the bike.

As I passed the turn off to Dun Aengus, I saw footprints in the snow and paused for a moment before following them in.

As I entered the old fort, a tall figure in a long black coat was standing on the cliff top, his coattails flapping in the wind. I approached cautiously; my footsteps muffled by the snow. He was standing close to the edge, and I was reluctant to call out lest I startle him. As I reached out to touch his shoulder he turned abruptly and almost stumbled over the edge. I grabbed his arm, realizing at that moment that it wasn't the old man, it was the priest.

"Jesus Aiden!" I was shocked, "What are you doing?"

"Conor!" Tears were streaming down his face "You should have let me go."

"No, mate!" I said, "Not like this."

"You don't know what it's like," he was sobbing uncontrollably, "I can't stop drinking, I just can't."

"I know exactly what it's like." I had a grip on his arm,

"Come over here, come on, out of the wind. We'll talk."

I led him away from the brink to the shelter of the wall. There was a campfire burning in a ring of stones, a few logs on the ground alongside.

"You lit this?" I asked.

"No."

We talked for two hours huddled around the fire. I told him my story; he told me his. His early days in the priesthood, the beliefs he'd once had. How he came to lose his faith.

"The more I doubted, the more I read." There were still tears on his cheeks, "First the Bible, then theology. I was convinced my salvation lay in learning. But then I realized one day that the more I read, the more I doubted. That's when I began trying to convince other people. It was as if I was trying to convince myself."

"How did you end up a priest, Aiden?"

"Oh, God!" He turned and looked out over the ocean, "My mother, God Bless her."

"She wanted you to be a priest?"

"Doesn't every Irish mother want her first son to be a priest? Or they did back then at least."

"How old are you?"

"I'll be thirty-seven come January."

"That's the same age I was when I got sober." I told him.

"She was a good woman," he raised his eyes to meet mine, "But a fierce Catholic. I never knew my father. He died shortly after I was born, tuberculosis. She brought up three children by herself. Not an easy task."

"And you were the oldest?"

"Yes, two boys and a girl. Sure she had me slated for the

priesthood before I could walk, God forgive her."

"So you weren't keen on the idea?"

"It's hard to say, when you're raised like that. There's an expectation, you don't question it. It's just there."

"But you must have considered other things by the time you were leaving school?"

"I did of course. Sure I met a girl at high school, Siobhan. That had me questioning the whole thing. But we'd already had a meeting with the bishop, and I'd been assigned a place in a seminary in Galway."

"So what happened to Siobhan?"

"My mother chased her off. Went around to her parent's house. God knows what was said, but I never saw her again."

"And you entered the seminary in Galway?"

"That's right, but they had me transferred to Dublin within days. Probably because of Siobhan."

"How was your time at the seminary?"

"Not good. But I knew if I left, it would break my mother's heart."

"What do you think you might have done if you hadn't become a priest?"

"Jaysus, what's the difference? Sure, I am a priest, it's too late now to change that."

"Aiden, you're on the point of being defrocked, thrown out. Is there a plan B?"

"God no. I have no idea at all of what I'd do. I've never given it a second thought."

"What are you good at? What do you enjoy doing? You read a lot; yes?"

"Yes, I've always loved reading. That's what I do up there

at the cottage. When I'm not on the drink that is."

"And you enjoy trying to help people; yes?"

"How's that?'

"Well, you seem to like preaching to people."

"Yes, but that's what priests do; is it not?"

"Aiden, you like to study, you enjoy helping people, you have a good sense of humour, and a way of expressing yourself that holds people's attention. Those are some of the gifts that I see in you."

"Where are you headed with this, Conor?"

"Look, you never wanted to be a priest, that's clear. You were coerced into it by your mother."

"Hold on now…"

"Stop, Aiden, just stop for a moment and hear me out. Your mother was a fine woman, and she meant nothing but the best for you; there's no denying that. She did what she thought was right. But it wasn't right for you. So, she's responsible for that, but she's not to blame; okay?"

"She was a great woman altogether; I was gutted when she passed."

"And you're still being loyal to her." I told him, "Even though it's clear that you're working in the wrong field."

"It's too late to change horses now, Conor!"

"No, it's not. I was an advertising executive in Australia when I fell apart. Now I'm halfway around the world building boats on the Aran Islands."

"So, what are you suggesting, that I leave the priesthood?"

"Do you honestly want to stay on as a priest for another twenty, thirty, or forty years? Is that something you'd look forward to?"

"God no!" He put his face in his hands and began weeping again. "Sure, I couldn't bear the thought."

"Okay, I think you have your answer. Look, we're going to work on this together. First, you're going to get sober. Next, we're going to find out exactly what your gifts are. After that, I'm going to help you discover what your purpose is in life; okay?"

He was staring at me.

"You're a Christian man, Conor?"

"I'm no idea what I am anymore. But I know there's a benevolent power in this world. And I know that power lifts us up when we get off our own case and reach out to others."

"How can I thank you?"

"There's no need," I told him. "I'm just passing it on."

"But do you think I can do it? Stay sober I mean?"

"It's Christmas Day." I told him, "It's the first day of the rest of your life. Go home, get cleaned up. Whatever you have at your place, booze, drugs, pills, chuck it all out. Eat something if you can, then get some rest." I gave him a hug, "Six o'clock tomorrow morning at the boatshed, okay?"

"Stay with me, Conor."

"I will, Aiden," I told him, "We're in this together."

I watched as he walked away, stumbling a little on the rocky ground. And when he reached the entranceway to the fort, he stopped, turned, and waved back at me. And within that simple gesture, I felt a great sense of hope.

EPILOGUE

AS I APPROACHED the boatshed, I found myself hoping there'd be smoke at the chimney, but there was not, and I knew in my heart he was gone.

I made tea, then sat in my chair looking around, smiling as I recalled the antics of the previous evening. It was then that I spotted the book. It was sitting on the brickwork that surrounds the fireplace and I wondered how I'm missed it when I first walked in. I went across and picked it up. It looked very old. A creased leather cover, no title, just the faded image of a triskele, imprinted on the leather in fine gold filigree. Ornate, like something the ancient monks might have used to embellish a biblical text. I opened the book. In the center of the first page in faded gold print, the words:

The Secret of Inis Mór

The paper was brittle and yellowed with age. I turned the page,

There are some who should read these words
and there are others who should not
If your life is ideal, and as you wish it to be
Then it may be better that you do not continue
Put this book aside or pass it on to another

For whoever reads these words
Their lives will be changed forever
and they will never be the same again.

I stared at the words for a long time, then I put the book in my pocket, closed the doors behind me, and walked back home to my wife and son.

The End

From the Author

Dear reader, if you enjoyed this book, I would be grateful if you took the time to leave a review on Amazon.com. Reviews like yours are extremely helpful to an author, and for that, I thank you in advance.

I have spent many memorable days on Inis Mór, and some of the characters in this book are based on real people from there. The two old sisters, Brigid, and Madge, I knew well and had tea in their kitchen many a time. No electricity, the water heated on an old, cast-iron stove top.

They were very much the island's historians and have only recently passed. As for the priest, I won't even hint as to his identity. I was 'fond of the drink' myself for many years and am not in any position to judge!

Another book is planned, and I hope to have it out by late 2024. My website details, which have all my books listed, are below. Please keep in touch, I will respond to all when I can.

And once again, thank you for all your kind reviews and comments,

Brian O'Raleigh
November 2023

brianoraleighbooks.com

THE FIRST BOOK IN THIS SERIES:

Passage to Inis Mór

Could a Legend Save a Life?

When 38-year-old Conner O'Rourke arrives in Ireland after an absence of thirty years, his life is in bits. His marriage is falling apart, his advertising agency in Australia is bankrupt, and he's hearing poetic voices in his mind urging him to return home to the Island of Inis Mór.

His grandmother has contacted him, saying that she is dying and must speak with him, but when he arrives on Inis Mór, a hauntingly lonely, starkly beautiful island in Galway Bay, she has already passed, leaving him a cottage and a dilapidated, old sailing boat.

A mysterious stranger appears, offering to help rebuild the boat and, as they work together, the old man tells Conner stories of Ireland. Stories of courage, purpose, and passion. Stories that could redeem Conner's lost integrity, if only he can muster the courage to follow his heart.

"Brian O'Raleigh's new book, *Passage to Inis Mór*, reminds one of the great Irish writers such as Sean O'Faolain and Benedict Kiely."
Frank O'Shea – Literary critic – *The Irish Echo*

Purchase at: tinyurl.com/4wu85m3j
brianoraleighbooks.com
reasonforbeing.com.au

Other books by Brian O'Raleigh

Return to Mór

Waiting for Walter. A Memoir

Waking Walter. Memoir – Part 2.

Passage to Inis Mór. A modern-day classic set on one of Ireland's most beautiful islands.

Coming soon!

The Secret of *Inis Mór*. *The final book in the Inis Mór series.* Late 2024

Endor's Way – a compelling murder mystery set between Bondi Beach, Australia, and the island of Inis Mór, Ireland. Available January 2024.

Frank O'Shea of the Irish Echo.
"O'Raleigh writing is very much in the tradition of Irish storytelling, with strong, vibrant prose that reminds of writers such as Sean O'Faolain and Benedict Kiely".

brianoraleighbooks.com
brianoraleighbooks@hotmail.com

Waiting for Walter

A Memoir

Growing up in his parent's hotel in Blackpool, Brian never knew why his parents fled Ireland. But he learned early to escape his father's demonic rages by slipping away from the Alexandra Private Hotel to the beach and the Kathleen R, the fishing boat that would become his refuge and his sanctuary.

At the age of eighteen, forced to flee the law in England, Brian travels throughout Europe, the war zones of the Middle East, and the mining towns of Australia, in a futile attempt to escape his own inner demons, the same demons that destroyed his father's life and caused his early death.

Waiting for Walter tells the riveting story of Brian's violent childhood, his descent into alcoholism and crime, his dramatic and inspirational recovery, and his passionate search for meaning and purpose. A quest that would ultimately lead him to the profound realization that it is only in discovering our true purpose in life can we hope to achieve happiness, fulfilment, and success.

The Australian Irish Echo.

"O'Raleigh is a convincing writer, and this book deserves ranking with Angela's Ashes. He mixes dialogue, narrative and reflection in a story that is always gripping, often scary and sometimes funny. He is searingly honest, and if this work can bring help to other tortured souls, he deserves great credit."

The Australian Woman's Day.

"From raw and compelling prose, a moving portrait emerges of Brian. From cowed child to fierce rebel and finally to an adult battling his own inner demons. This is a finely crafted memoir."

Endor's Way

(Not for the faint hearted! Available January 2024)

CHAPTER 1

Bondi Beach

THE BODY WASHED up on Bondi Beach around 3.am, the time of arrival established by its presence amongst the flotsam and jetsam that marked the furthest extent of the incoming tide. Empty beer bottles, old tennis balls, and multi-colored plastic thongs lay scattered recklessly along the high-water mark, intertwined with seaweed, bits of rope and the odd piece of driftwood. Rejected, along with Jameson, hurled back from whence they came by an angry, disillusioned ocean.

He'd been a handsome man, but as he lay there face up waiting for a savior now long overdue, you could never have guessed that. The crabs and little fish that had escorted him on his long, slow drift from the foot of the cliffs at North Head to his final resting place on the beach at Bondi, had been pulling at the edges of the gaping chest wound that had terminated his life.

I arrived at the beach around eight o'clock it was a miserable day, grey clouds hurrying furtively across a darkening sky and the wind, coming in from the south-east, keening over the ocean swells like a requiem for lost souls.

The early morning jogger who'd stumbled across the body

just before dawn was being questioned by the local police just out of the weather near the entrance to the surf club. I glanced at her as I got out of the car. She was around forty-five or so, tall, blond, and skinny, her arms folded tightly across a Spandex plated, anorexic chest, still pale and visibly shaken from her grisly find.

I nodded to the sergeant and moved past them towards the beach. Another half a dozen uniforms were on the windswept sands, close by the wading pool. Two of them were on their knees, securing the flapping yellow tape that determined where the public stopped and started; beyond that a small crowd of vultures in anoraks and track-suit pants hovered, drawn in by the scent of death, eager to be part of the unfolding drama.

As I approached the main group, the uniforms parted to reveal the kneeling figure of Carl Seagan, doctor, coroner, and if his detractors were correct, one-time abortionist to the Sydney social set. As he recognized me, his face took on a slight frown.

"Glad you managed to make it before the tide came back in, Harrigan," he turned back to the body.

Before I could respond, his assistant, a worried-looking young man just out of medical school, fumbled…

"I'm sorry, sir, it's your partner. It's Detective Jameson …"

Email:
brianoraleighbooks@hotmail.com

Website:
brianoraleighbooks.com

All Brian's books are available on Amazon and Kindle

Printed in Great Britain
by Amazon